Tempest in a Blaze of Glory

a Shiiloh Tempest novel

David Hunter

Tempest in a Blaze of Glory

Copyright © 2021 by David Hunter

All rights reserved. No part of this book may be reproduced or transmitted in any form or by any means without written permission of the author.

Printed in the United States of America.

Oconee Spirit Press, Waverly, TN www.oconeespirit.com

978-0-9984940-4-3

Library of Congress Cataloging-in-Publication Data

Hunter, David. Tempest in a Blaze of Glory.

p.cm.

This is a work of fiction. All of the characters, organizations, and events portrayed in this novel are either products of the author's imagination or are used fictitiously.

1.Police – Tennessee - Fiction. 2. Knoxville (Tenn.) – Fiction. 3. Tempest, Shiloh (Fictitious character).

The text paper is SFI certified. The Sustainable Forestry Initiative® program promotes sustainable forest management.

Cover design by Dead Center

Cover image © Karencampbell| Dreamstime.com

Once again, this book is dedicated to my wife, Cheryl Krooss Hunter.

ONE

The thoughts of my own mortality first entered my mind as I drove my cruiser across the Henley Street Bridge, over the Tennessee River, with the Knoxville-Knox County City-County Building to my right and the Sunsphere, left over from the 1982 World's Fair, to my left. At least that's the first time I remember dwelling on my mortality.

How good would the ten thousandth bowl of cherry cobbler with vanilla ice cream taste? How long would my damaged and often pain-wracked body allow me to make love to my beautiful *compañera*, Jennifer?

Would she be able to keep the house, even on her salary as a successful attorney? We have never married, because she had a horrible first marriage. *Did I want to leave things unfinished as they are between us?*

True, by age fifty-nine, I had achieved much in my dual careers as a writer and a cop, with two *New York Times* bestsellers and becoming Chief Deputy of the Knox County Sheriff's Office.

Maybe it was age itself that was bothering me. I have lived my life through a lot of precarious situations. As a soldier, then a street cop, I've flirted with death hundreds of times.

Actually, I had always thought I'd go out in a blaze of glory like in the early 1980s song popularized by Kenny Rogers. Yet, here I am pushing sixty, with my body growing more battered all the time.

I quickly shook off the feeling, or so I thought at the time.

Jennifer's car was parked outside the garage and I saw her looking out the kitchen window. A second later, I saw our German shepherd, Magdala, also looking out, feet on the window sill, ears at attention. Then she disappeared and I knew she would be at the inside garage door waiting.

Just as expected, I heard Magdala sniffing under the door with the power of an air compressor, whimpering between snorts. When I opened the door, our mostly-black German shepherd was dancing around my legs.

"Hello, Magdala." I stopped and caught her head between my palms, massaging her ears. "How's the girl?" She moaned deeply from her chest. It doesn't take a lot to make Magdala happy.

"*Hola, señor policía*," Jennifer said, following Magdala to the kitchen door. "Do you mind if I kiss my lover, Magdala?"

Magdala sat obediently and Jennifer kissed me lightly on the lips. She was wearing a yellow terrycloth robe and her long black hair was pulled back in a ponytail.

"Have you eaten, Shy?"

"No, I've been busy."

"Busy, doing what, *mi amor*?" She turned, opened the refrigerator, and took out a sandwich box from Firehouse Subs. "I bought you a New York Steamer, just in case." Magdala was instantly alert.

"Mostly thinking, Jen. I do it best in my cruiser."

"I know," she said, handing me a bottled Diet Dr. Pepper.

"Did John Freed reach you?"

"No, does he need me to call him?"

"He said you could talk in the morning. I got the distinct impression he wanted to ask *me* a question. But whatever it was, he couldn't get it out."

"That redheaded detective is shy and you intimidate him," I replied, taking the soft drink and sandwich from Jennifer. "Walk to the bedroom with me so I can get out of these clothes and relax with my dinner."

"I *intimidate* John? We're friends."

"You intimidate most men, Love. Beauty, brains, and a law degree to boot. Takes a real man to cohabit with you."

"You're so humble, Shy. Let me take your jacket off." I put the Dr. Pepper and sandwich on my bedside table, and she helped me out of my dark blue sports jacket. "Magdala, stop sniffing at Shy's dinner."

I loosened my tie and took it off, then shed my shirt and khaki slacks. Jennifer took them and put them on hangers.

"Shy, why do you insist on plaid shirts? You never wear any of the nice pastels I buy for you."

"Plaid shirts and solid ties are my trademark." I sat on the bed and reached for my sandwich.

"At least I got you to stop wearing those knit ties that went out of style years ago."

"You threw them away," I said

"That's true. I just want you to be a little more stylish."

"I'll ask Freed what he wanted tomorrow." I changed the subject. "Jen..." I hesitated...

"Yes, Shy?"

"We've been together for twenty years. To me that's an indication that we are a fairly good match. Do you ever think about letting me make an honest woman of you?"

"Shy, I'm *already* an honest woman. Why are you bringing this up again after so many years?"

"I really don't know, Jen. It was just on my mind earlier."

"Do we need to talk, Shy? I didn't know it was bothering you."

"No, we *don't* need to talk—and it's not bothering me. It was just a passing thought." I retreated from the subject and she seemed willing to accept it, for the moment.

TWO

The house phone began to ring as Jennifer came into the bedroom and put a cup of coffee on my bedside table. She was wearing black panties and bra and walking around with bare feet. I stopped to watch her crossing the room. After twenty years together, she can still take away my breath.

"Did I ever tell you...?"

"That I look like Madeline Stowe from that ancient movie *Stakeout*? Yes, about ten thousand times. Are you going to answer the phone?"

"It's my agent, Freddy. He's the only person who ever calls from New York," I said, sitting up against the padded headboard of our bed. I took a sip of coffee and savored it.

"Is this Jamaican Blue?" I asked.

"No, it's a blend from Hawaii. Answer the damn phone, Shy."

With my best theatrical sigh, I picked up the phone. "Chief Deputy Shiloh Tempest of the Knox County Sheriff's Office. Go ahead."

Freddy Shirk was momentarily startled into silence. I knew he would be wondering if he had called my office, because Freddy is very organized but easily distracted.

"Shy...?"

"Who did you call, Freddy?"

"I called you, but I thought I was calling your home, not your office."

"I'm the same person at both numbers, Freddy."

"It's not too early, is it? I can never remember the time difference."

"Freddy, unless they've moved New York City since the last time you called, there is no time difference. I'm in Tennessee not Europe. Now, if you call Nashville, it's an hour earlier there."

"Why do you always mess with my mind, Shy? Sometimes I think you don't even like me."

"Because it's so easy, Freddy. But I love you, anyway. What did you need to talk to me about?"

"I had a call from your editor about your use of the word *roué* in your new novel."

"*Roué*, from the French, 'a debauched or lecherous person, generally an elderly man', from the Latin *rex*.' It's a perfectly good word, Freddy."

"I'm sure it is, Shy, but Libby says it doesn't sound right coming from the mouth of a hard-boiled homicide detective."

"Freddy, I know she wants me to change it. I got her e-mail and I said *no*. What part of that doesn't Libby understand?" I said, taking another sip of coffee.

"Shy, did you really send back an e-mail to Libby that said, *Writers write; editors edit*?"

"Yes, I did. As you recall, we included the clause that says the publisher can't make a change, other than spelling or to correct punctuation *without my permission*."

"I'm sure they didn't think you'd be *unreasonable*, Shy," Freddy said, letting a pitiful edge creep into his voice. He hates confrontation.

"Freddy, I think they were unreasonable with that paltry advance they gave us on this last book. Tell them if they're not happy with the product, we can renegotiate or they can release me and take back their miserable advance."

"Shy, you've always said it's not *just* about the money."

"It's *not* just about the money, Freddy, but most writers I know with my track record are getting much bigger advances. I don't like being taken for granted."

"Well, I'll get back with Libby." Freddy was almost whimpering.

"Do that, Freddy. And be prepared for when she gets to the place where my detective yells *gardyloo* to warn another cop to duck or be shot. It's an obsolete interjection used in medieval Scotland before people had indoor plumbing to warn passers-by that a chamber pot was about to be emptied out from a window."

Freddy came pretty close to slamming down the phone. That's one of the advantages of having an older phone like Freddy's. You can use it to vent frustration. The sound was louder than usual, but not quite a slam.

"What in the world was that about, Shy?" Jennifer paused in brushing her long dark hair. "You always razz Freddy—but a dispute with an editor?"

"Maybe I have decided to assert myself more," I answered.

"Like you *need* to be more assertive," Jennifer said.

THREE

I was on my way up to the administrative offices of Knox County government, which are on the sixth floor of the Knox County City-County Building. The structure was completed in the late 1970s and those who were opposed to the project are still waiting for the building to topple off the ridge upon which it is built, above the Tennessee River.

The flat areas of the city had been used up long before the building was raised, but it is still holding up well.

The personnel office for Knox County government is at the end of a long hallway on the northwest side of the City-County Building.

It has always seemed ironic to me that an incoming employee goes to the top floor and walks down a long hallway to sign in on the first day, then makes the same trip on termination or retirement day. Of course, I'm a writer and I see irony where most people don't.

Pushing the door open, I went in and saw JoAnn Silver, who had been there before I pinned on my first badge as a reserve deputy sheriff who worked for free. Her kinky blonde hair had turned white through the years, but the way she styled it had not changed.

"Shiloh Tempest," she said with a smile, "you have barely changed in the three decades since you first walked through that door."

"Liar," I said. "You're the one who hasn't changed—same 1980s permanent, just a different color."

"Shiloh, I've been telling you for thirty years, my hair is *naturally* curly. Dad always said we have a touch of African genes, and this ain't no white girl butt."

She stood, slapped her bottom, and walked to the counter. "Now what can I do for the chief deputy?"

"For one thing, you can begin by stifling racial and sexist comments. We aren't in the seventies any longer."

She looked at me as if puzzled, trying to read my face to see if I was serious. I laughed and gave it away. "Gotcha," I said.

"The thing is, you're right," she said with a shake of her head. "I'm a dinosaur, I guess. Now what did you need?"

"I want to make Jennifer my sole beneficiary."

"How is the lovely Jennifer?" JoAnn asked.

"She's good, and I'll tell her you asked about her."

I waited as JoAnn pulled up my account on the computer.

"Shiloh, your son has been your sole beneficiary since he was born. Why the change?"

Realizing that she had mixed a longstanding personal relationship with business, her cheeks flushed. "Sorry, that was none of my business."

"No problem, JoAnn. I trust Jennifer to do what I would do. My son's ultra-conservative grandfather has more money than King Midas and has spoiled him to the extreme. He'll be well taken care of, even if I leave nothing. Jen's my first priority."

"I remember. Jen had a horrible marriage. Has it really been more than twenty years since my husband and I dined with you and Jennifer at Los Charros?"

"It has. Los Charros is ancient history and my health isn't the best. Things change rapidly sometimes."

"Your heart isn't acting up again, is it?"

"No more than usual, just tying up loose ends, JoAnn, so Jen won't have to handle things alone—if something happens to me. I have a hazardous job, you know."

On my way down, I exited the elevator to buy a pack of cigarettes. It's the floor shared by the District Attorney, generally called the Attorney General in Tennessee and many of the courts. The coffee shop, where cigarettes are sold, is on the same floor.

As I approached the front door of the coffee shop, Al Reagan who had taken my old job as Chief of Detectives when I moved up to Chief Deputy was exiting and he held the door open.

"Chief, we need to talk," said Reagan, a big balding bear of a man with wire-rimmed glasses, who looks more like a construction laborer than a detective.

"OK, *Chief*," I replied. "Sit with me while I have a cup of coffee."

"This is serious, Shy. Don't be facetious." To Al, everything is serious.

"Get us a table, Al, and I'll get my coffee; and when we talk I'll be as non-facetious as possible."

When I sat down at the table with coffee for both of us, I found Reagan polishing his glasses with the special papers he carries with him.

I've noticed that the frequency of polishing the lenses goes down when Al falls off the wagon and starts smoking. A recovering smoker has to keep his hands occupied.

"This looks serious, Al," I said. "Maybe a two polishing paper matter."

"You said you would take this seriously, Shy."

"Sorry, Al. Let's have it." I took a swig of my black coffee with two artificial sweeteners. It used to be real sugar, but my doctor had become dissatisfied with my blood sugar levels. He and Jennifer had teamed up against me.

"Todd Aiken has been released from the Veterans Administration psychiatric ward in Murfreesboro where they put him after he tried to kill you the last time." He paused for dramatic effect.

"Maybe he's cured, and even if he's not, that ass whipping John Freed gave him when he sneaked into my hospital room will stay with him a long time. It was hard to believe that skinny shy redhead had so much violence in him."

"We both know better, Shy. Aiken's delusional and dangerous. He probably stopped his meds when they let him out yesterday."

"How did you learn about this, Al? I haven't seen any paperwork on it."

"Sheriff Renfro told me about it as soon as he got here this morning. One of his friends told him about it last night. So what do you plan on doing to improve your security?"

"Al, I work in an office full of cops; there's a pistol within grabbing distance, even when I'm in bed, and a one-hundred-pound German shepherd sleeps on the floor between my bed and the bedroom door. I'm as safe as I can be and do my job."

"Aiken almost killed you in the sheriff's office garage, Shy, then tried again while you were in the hospital."

"Yes. I remember. I was there when it happened. That's because he worked building security for the City-County Building and had keys to every door in the building, Al."

"I think you need a security detail, and so does the Sheriff."

"Al, if Aiken threatens me again, he will find Hell coming after him." Al's eyes opened wide and I immediately said, "I can't believe I just said that."

"I think Wyatt Earp said something like that once," Al said.

"I saw the movie, Al. *Tombstone* is one of my favorite films. That's where it probably came from. It didn't sound like something I would say."

"You're right about that, Chief. You're not big on primate strutting."

"Oh well, I'll have to fight with the Sheriff over this, I guess, because he'll tell Jennifer and they will gang up on me. So I'd better get my day started."

FOUR

When I arrived at the entrance to the sheriff's office, Detective John Freed was waiting in the lobby. A tall, lanky redhead with the alabaster complexion Southern belles once longed for.

Freed was obviously agitated. The boy is nervous as a cat in a roomful of rocking chairs by nature.

"Chief, Sheriff Renfro wants to see you," the receptionist said. A beautiful girl with hair like my Jennifer, Cheryl Tappet almost always had a group of young men hanging around her desk. Most would have been surprised to know she prefers women to men as bed partners.

"I'll get with him as soon as I talk to Detective Freed, Cheryl. I believe he has been waiting a while."

"Please do, Chief." She turned and looked at John mischievously. "John has turned me into a nervous wreck by just sitting there, fidgeting."

"Let's go to my office, John." The tall thin detective smiled at Cheryl and got up.

Inside my office, I poured myself a cup of coffee that had been prepared by my secretary, Holly Sowers. I had told her repeatedly that I could make my own coffee, but finally gave up. She had decided it was a duty that belonged within her domain.

"John, grab yourself a soft drink out of my little fridge." Freed does not drink coffee.

"That's all right, Chief. I need to get to work. There's something I want to run by you. If you don't think it's a good idea, I won't be offended. So..."

"Spit it out, John."

"CJ and I would like to have our wedding at your house." He swallowed and his Adam's apple went up and down, then his pale skin flushed. "Just a small group of people—what CJ calls an *intimate* affair."

"How *intimate* do we have to get, John?"

"Well, you know... not *intimate* intimate. What he meant..." Freed paused and grinned. "You're jerking me around, aren't ya, Chief?"

"Not in an *intimate* sense, John. Is this what you wanted to ask Jennifer about? She said you wanted to say something but never got up the courage."

"Yeah. You know, I'm more afraid of her than you, Chief. Not that she's ever been anything but kind... She's... you know..."

"She's *intimidating*, John."

"Yeah, she is. Don't tell her I said that, Chief, I wouldn't want to hurt her feelings."

"Relax, John. The hard part's over now. I'd be honored to host your wedding—but you *will* have to work out the details with Jennifer. And John, she scares me, too. Mostly because I still don't know why she picked me to be her bed-mate twenty years ago."

"I can't wait to tell, CJ. He will be *so* excited to have my friends give their blessing to our marriage. It's not always like that for people like us, you know."

"You mean tall handsome men, John?"

He started to speak, but smiled and shook his head ruefully. I saw tears in his eyes.

"I know, John. I know."

FIVE

After John left my office, I checked my e-mail and voice mail, then picked up the messages Holly had stacked neatly on the edge of my desk.

Better get the meeting with the sheriff out of the way, I thought just as there was a knock on my office door.

"Come in."

"Since the mountain wouldn't come to Mohammed, Mohammed has come to the mountain," said Sheriff Renfro, as he entered my office.

"Sorry, Sam. I've had things going on."

"But I *am* the High Sheriff, used to being catered to."

"Yeah, I've seen you high a few times when you were *simulating* a few tokes of the wacky weed."

"Do you think anyone ever believed that *simulating* bull shit?" Sam is right at six feet tall, dressed sharply and with his dark hair trimmed neatly.

We had once called him the chameleon because of his ability to assume the identity of a drug dealer. Legend has it that when he was undercover, a drug dealer had once refused to even talk to "that nasty looking piece of shit."

"I don't know, Sheriff, but you were always very convincing."

"I'm pretty good at being a convincing sheriff, too, except to my Chief Deputy, who takes my orders as suggestions."

"All right, Sam, I get the message—be more subservient to the sheriff. I'll write it down. What did you need, Exalted One?"

"I didn't *need* anything, Hoss. Just going to invite an old friend to lunch—assuming you can make time for me."

I had been prepared to argue about the extra security Al Reagan and the sheriff had already discussed, but mentally shifted gears.

"It's a little early for lunch, Sam."

"That's all right. I have a short stop on the way to Puleo's, where you can get the fried green tomatoes you like so much.

"We can kill a little time smoking one of your cigarettes." He pulled a chair from the side of the desk, straddled it backwards as if mounting a horse, and faced me.

Sam had given up smoking years ago, except when the two of us are alone. He keeps an ashtray in his desk drawer, usually for times of stress—of which I am very often the cause.

I took out my Camel filters, and extended the pack to him and took out my own ashtray from the desk drawer.

Smoking is now forbidden throughout the City-County Building, but even if someone saw him smoking it was unlikely they would say anything.

"Got a light, Bubba?"

I tossed my butane throwaway lighter to him. He lit his cigarette, slid the lighter back across the desk, and waited until I lit up.

"How about them Vols?" he asked.

"You know I don't keep up with sports, Sam."

"Sorry, it's just a reflex. Almost every man in East Tennessee at least *pretends* to be up to the minute with University of Tennessee football."

"Yeah, I'm a failure as a Southern male. I never have owned a pick-up truck; don't hunt or fish and drink very little beer."

"And don't forget, you also eat quiche and arugula. You're a disgrace to Southern manhood for sure."

We pulled out of the garage in Sam's unmarked silver Oldsmobile, turning right on Main Street then left on Gay Street, which had been the main drive and center of business before strip malls popped up all over Knoxville. Almost immediately, Sam slowed down and moved to the curb.

"Would you look at that beautiful woman standing by the curb," Sam said. "I think I'll try to pick her up."

Jennifer, my gorgeous *compañera*, smiled and moved to the curb as she spotted us.

"I should have known," I said. "You and Jen are going to take me to lunch and beat up on me until I agree to a security detail."

"Let Jen sit in the middle," Sam said. "Let's face it, Bubba, I'm the High Sheriff of Knox County. I don't need your permission to assign you a security detail. I just enjoy being seen in the company of one of the most beautiful women I know. If you like, I'll take you back to the office and have Jen to myself for lunch."

"All right, you're the Sheriff and I'm just your Chief Deputy. You are going to do as you wish anyway. I'll just eat my fried green tomatoes while you and my wife make decisions concerning my life. Why should today be any different than any other?"

Jennifer—less than a wife, but more than a companion—got into the cruiser and Sam immediately began to openly flirt with her.

I often told Jen that if I checked out, Sam would be at the front door waiting. I was only half joking.

Sam took I-40 West from the downtown exit, then immediately switched to I-75 North. The traffic situation isn't great but it is better than the mess once called "Malfunction Junction" it had replaced.

Ten minutes later, he exited left on Merchant Drive, and Puleo's Grille was only a few blocks away.

Puleo's is a small Tennessee chain that markets itself as an "Italian-Southern United States fusion." The menu runs from traditional spaghetti and lasagna, to fish tacos and fried green tomatoes, which are available all year.

They know me at Puleo's because I occasionally do a foodie column for local papers and have written about them. "Your usual booth, Chief Tempest?" A young woman with a Modigliani like neck asked.

"That will be fine, Teresa."

The young hostess escorted us to the back of the restaurant and the booth from which I could see everyone who entered the building. She left us with menus and quietly retreated.

"Man, oh man," Sam said. "the High Sheriff enters a restaurant and they suck up to his deputy."

"Who is also a bestselling author and a by God folk hero." I said. "You can't be the center of attention all the time, Sheriff Showboat."

"Both of you over-sized infants turn down the *machismo*. Don't make me take you outside for a talk," Jennifer said.

Jen and Sam each ordered filet mignon with a baked potato and Caesar salad. I ordered fried green tomatoes over grits, normally an appetizer, along with

15

Puleo's red and white chili on the side, then enjoyed my meal while my *compañera* and best friend planned my security detail.

I do love fried green tomatoes.

SIX

Sam dropped me off at the front door of the City-County building, telling me he had a "business appointment," which I took to mean a few rounds of golf. In actuality, more deals are made by men over lunch or on a golf course than ever take place in an office. Most men, that is. I don't play golf, either.

One of the deputies working security at a table inside the front door — a big husky boy who appeared to be a weightlifter—waved me past the metal detector. "Come on in, Chief."

There are a lot of fit young men in the department these days. When I started, most of us were pale from too little sunlight, at least on the night shift where the action is, and sat in roll call smoking cigarettes and drinking coffee. The times have changed.

Standing in the hallway in front of the building security office, Detective John Freed was nose to nose with Todd Aiken, my attempted assassin.

John, tall and thin—"wiry" as he referred to himself—was leaning down to get in the face of the husky Aiken, the former security officer and Army Ranger.

"You have a lot of nerve sashaying in here and asking to see Chief Shiloh Tempest after you tried to kill him *twice*." Freed's face was red.

"John, fill me in please," I said.

The detective stopped, startled for a second, then looked at me.

"Just debating with Mister Aiken about him showing up the day after he left the loony bin and asking for you."

"Bring him back to my office, John. He had to walk through the metal detector to get in."

"He may still have keys, Chief."

"Then pat him down and bring him back to my office, John."

"On the wall, Aiken," John said. The former security officer complied without protest, and I walked by them and entered the lobby of the sheriff's offices.

"What's the ruckus out in the hallway, Chief?" the receptionist asked.

"It was John Freed having a difference of opinion with a man who tried to kill me twice."

"I've never heard John Freed raise his voice," the striking brunette receptionist said.

"There's more to John than the casual eye sees. Look at the guy John is bringing through. Our mild-mannered detective almost beat him to death when he tried to kill me the last time, while calling him vile names."

I unlocked my office, hung up my coat, and poured myself a cup of coffee. A moment later, John and Aiken were at the door.

"Come in." I said.

Aiken entered the office and John followed him closely. The short stocky, blond former security officer and Army Ranger stood respectfully in front of my desk.

"Detective Freed, that will be all," I said. The expression on Freed's face told me I'd have to suspend him if I tried to enforce my order. Freed is absolutely loyal and dedicated to protecting me.

"Very well, John—then close the door."

John complied, keeping his eyes on Aiken.

"How can I help you, Mister Aiken?" I asked.

"I was pretty messed up the last time we saw each other..." he began.

"You think so?" Freed said.

"John..."

Freed pursed his lips but went silent.

"Go ahead, Mister Aiken. Say what you wanted to say."

"I wanted to *apologize*. I was delusional and having a psychotic break when I tried to hurt you before."

"Is that all?" I asked.

"Yes."

"All right, Mister Aiken—but understand this. You come after me again and there won't just be another ass whipping like John gave you. If I even *suspect* you're a threat to me or my friends and family, I will personally *end* you. Do you understand?"

Freed's eyes widened at my words.

"I do," Aiken said.

"All right, you can leave. Be wise." I picked up a file and started reading.

"You've been dismissed, Aiken," Freed said. "Understand that if you threaten Shiloh Tempest again and I get to you first..."

Aiken nodded and opened the door to leave. A tall, blond and muscular uniformed sergeant by the name of Larry Wilkin was standing outside the door.

He stepped back to let Aiken pass, looking the shorter man up and down. "Is everything all right here?"

"We're good, Wilkin. Why did you think there was a problem?" I asked.

The sergeant shrugged. "Well you know how the grapevine works, Chief."

"Miss Tappet from the front desk told you to look in, didn't she?"

"Yes sir."

"Thanks for your concern, Sergeant Wilkin," I said.

"Yeah, we appreciate it," Freed said.

"Detective Freed," Wilkin said, "I hear you're getting married. When are you going to bring your fiancée by to meet us?"

"In due time," Freed replied.

Wilkin nodded and walked away.

"How did he know about your upcoming marriage, John?"

"Chief, there *is* quite a grapevine here. Most likely one of the girls in records told somebody else I had been talking about getting married and was asking how to plan a small wedding."

"That's good, John, just wondered."

"Everything is copacetic, Chief. Maybe I'll see you tonight," Freed said.

"You're off tonight, John."

"I volunteered to help stake out your house first shift tonight," Freed said.

"John..." I began, but he was gone before I could protest.

After John left, I saw that my secretary had left a stack of papers on my desk. The top sheet was a bid sheet for the position of Lieutenant with an expiration date of the next day.

Bill Blakely, who was the direct supervisor over half the detectives, was retiring.

I made a notation for my secretary, Holly, to put John on the interview list, even though he had not placed a bid. I knew he had taken the lieutenant's exam a couple of years earlier and the rank of detective is sergeant.

John would try to avoid being promoted because good cops like to stay in the field, but the tall redhead would be a solid addition to my supervisory staff.

As I finished initialing the stack of papers on my desk, Miss Tibbet spoke to me over the intercom: "Line two, Chief."

I picked up. "Chief Tempest," I said.

"It always gives me a thrill to hear you announce yourself as *jefe*" Jennifer said. "Sounds so authoritative.

"You rebuked me for being too macho not very long ago," I said.

"That was different, *mi amor*. Besides, a woman can change her mind."

"That's true, Love. Now give me the bad news."

"Not that bad, Shiloh. I'm going to be running a little late tonight. Can you pick up burgers or some other sandwich on the way home? And don't forget a children's order for Magdala."

"Where do you want me to stop?" I asked.

"Surprise me, *mi amor*. Have to go. I love you."

At that moment, there was a knock on my office door, the one that led directly into the hallway.

"Come in," I said, knowing it had to be someone I knew, else they would have had to get past my secretary.

The door opened and a tall black man, thirty or so, with a shaved head and spiffily dressed—a Denzel Washington look-a-like—entered the office.

"What's happening, Chief of Detectives Shiloh Tempest?"

"What's up with you, Knoxville Police Department Criminal Investigator Tom Abernathy? Sit down and I'll get you a cup of coffee."

Tom Abernathy had been the lead investigator from the Knoxville Police Department when my old friend and fellow cop Jerry Carpenter had been mutilated, murdered, and his body dumped at the base of Knoxville's Sunsphere.

His boss, the KPD Chief and old enemy of mine, had put Abernathy temporarily back in uniform to punish him for becoming close to me, even after the case was solved.

We had even checked on something called a lateral transfer for Tom to the Knox County Sheriff's Office, but it would have cost him too much in money and benefits.

"Black with one sugar, right, Tom?"

"You have a good memory, Shiloh."

"What brings you by, Tom?"

"Just a record's check on one of my dirtbag suspects," he said. "You know, sometimes I think about how things might have been if I had actually transferred over here."

"Well, you're welcome any time," I said.

"So what's happening over here, Shiloh?"

"Well, Todd Aiken is back on the street, out of the Veterans hospital at Murfreesboro. And John Freed is marrying his roommate, CJ, very soon."

"Well good for John," Abernathy said, draining his coffee cup. "Let me know if there's anything I can do to help you out."

"Same here, Tom, it was good to see you again."

I left the office around seven, picked up my old maroon-colored unmarked Ford cruiser and headed north towards my home in Powell, Tennessee, a suburb of Knoxville. As chief deputy, I could have had a brand-new cruiser, but I had always believed the working cops were entitled to the best equipment.

Not many years earlier the Powell community had been rural, but the city had almost caught up with me.

I resisted the temptation to make a second visit to Puleo's on Merchant Drive for another order of fried green tomatoes for me and burgers for Jennifer and Magdala, and drove on two more exits and got off at Emory Road.

I had a broad choice of places specializing in burgers, so I turned into the nearest one, a place called Billy's Burgers, where I knew I could get a burger with jalapeño slices and one with mushrooms for Jennifer.

I didn't notice that changes had been made to the parking places since I was last there, so I pulled up to the side door where I usually parked and went in.

I went to the counter and was greeted by a cheerful young woman with dark hair streaked in purple. "What can I get for you, Detective?"

"You must have seen the blue light on my dashboard," I said, "You're very perceptive." She dimpled up.

"I'll have a mushroom burger, a jalapeño burger, and a child's hamburger, plain, and two orders of onion rings," I told her.

As I stood waiting on my order, I was approached by a pudgy six-footer, maybe in his early twenties, wearing a white shirt with a pin that read 'Assistant Manager.' He was followed by a smaller man carrying cleaning supplies.

"Since you didn't notice, or think you're special," he said to me, "the spaces on this side of the building have been turned into part of the drive through lane. I'll have to ask you to move your car."

He spoke in a loud voice and glanced around the room to see if his act of authority had been noted by his employees. I looked and sure enough, the parking lanes had been striped out, but I hadn't noticed, being the only customer on the lot.

"Young lady," I said to the clerk who had taken my order, "cancel my order. I'll go to a place where the *assistant* manager has been trained in the art of courtesy."

I started to step past the hulking assistant manager, but he blocked my way. His face had become flushed. He took a step backwards and leaned forward to look down at me.

"So you do think *you're* special, *little man?*"

"You have no idea, you swaggering, Napoleonic idiot, how much slack I have already cut you because of your obvious ignorance. Now move out of my way."

Confusion passed briefly over his meaty face, probably because he was perplexed about being called *Napoleonic*, then he raised his hand and tapped me in the chest with his right index finger. "Let me tell you..."

I caught his hand, my index finger digging into a spot between his wrist and hand, then stepped slightly forward, turning his hand toward him with just enough force to bring tears to his eyes without causing his knees to buckle. He gasped in pain.

"You just crossed the line between rudeness and assault," I said. "There were many ways you could have politely pointed out my mistake, but you decided to swagger over here and impress the other employees with your authority. *Right?*"

He nodded affirmatively and grunted as I increased the pressure just a little.

"I am about to release your hand, after which you will say, 'I'm sorry, sir.' If you don't, I will cause you to experience pain and humiliation such as you didn't know existed. Hopefully, you will have learned that actions have consequences."

I released his hand and stood waiting. He took a deep breath, then stood for a second as if thinking about defying me.

"Well?" I said, "is school over? I'm waiting."

He took a deep breath and choked out, "I'm sorry, sir," then turned and quickly walked to the back.

I was pulling into Arby's parking lot when I heard the dispatcher say, *"Adam 1, see the man at Billy's Burger on Emory Road. He's requesting a supervisor regarding an alleged assault by a Knox County detective."*

Seconds later, I heard my Chief of Detectives, Al Reagan, tell the dispatcher to cancel the patrol supervisor because he would be handling the complaint himself.

Until that moment I had forgotten that an officer, probably John Freed, was tailing me as a part of my security detail and had, no doubt, witnessed the event at Billy's Burgers and immediately called Al Reagan on his cell phone.

Well, hell, I thought. I decided to buy Reagan a large roast beef because I knew I'd be seeing him shortly.

Magdala danced around the kitchen, torn between greeting me and the sandwich she knew was in the bag for her. Jennifer had put the food on the counter and stood as if puzzled.

"Who is the extra sandwich for?" she asked.

"Al Reagan," I said.

"You invited Al to the house for a roast beef sandwich at this hour?"

"No, but he'll be here shortly."

As if on cue, the headlights of my Chief of Detectives' unmarked unit hit the kitchen wall as he pulled into the driveway.

Jennifer walked over and opened the kitchen door from the garage and Al looked startled as she did.

"What would you like to drink with your sandwich, Al? I have bottled water, beer, and soft drinks," Jen said.

Al blinked behind his rimless glasses. "A soft drink would be nice," he said.

"Dr. Pepper, Coke, or a lemon-lime?"

"A Dr. Pepper, please," Al said. He was wearing blue jeans, a pullover shirt, and a Fraternal Order of Police windbreaker rather than his usual suit.

Magdala had given up her desire to be a good hostess and began to whimper for her sandwich.

"Settle down, Magdala." Jennifer picked up Magdala's bowl and began to tear the sandwich into pieces.

"Have a seat, Al." I picked up one of my two sliders and took a bite of roast beef and jalapeño. I pushed his large roast beef across the table.

"I'm dying to know the reason for your visit, Al—glad as I am to see you," Jen said.

"Well," Al said, "I just handled a complaint about a Knox County detective roughing up an assistant manager at Billy's Burgers…"

"What actually happened was, I restrained a pompous ass after he assaulted me," I said, taking another bite of my slider and a sip of my Dr. Pepper.

"*Shy*, tormenting your agent and arguing with your editor is bad enough, but now you're roughing up assistant managers at fast food places? What's *wrong* with you?"

"Jennifer…" Al cleared his throat. "Shiloh was technically right. The young man poked your roommate in the chest, which is assault. After I explained this to the assistant manager and reminded *his* boss that the Knox County Sheriff's Office provides escorts to the bank when they make night deposits, they decided to drop the matter."

Jennifer sighed. "Eat your sandwich, Al. My husband and I will discuss this later. I'm sorry you had to get out of bed to bail out your boss from this childish incident."

Magdala looked up from her food dish and whimpered. She understood the tone in Jennifer's voice as well as I did.

"Guess I'll take my roast beef and Dr. Pepper and be on my way," Al said, "and let you two talk things out." He picked up his sandwich and soft drink and made a quick exit.

"Well," Jennifer said, "are you going to explain roughing up a civilian over a nonsensical slight to your ego?"

"No, and furthermore, if the assistant manager *hadn't* apologized, I would have arrested him for assault. I don't think a further explanation is required."

Jennifer's eyes went dark and Magdala whimpered, because she understands body language as well as vocal tones.

SEVEN

I quietly got out of bed before Jennifer was awake, dressed, let Magdala out to relieve herself and left, with my dog whimpering about the change in routine.

My *compañera* and I had gone to sleep angry for the first time in a long while. It had happened only a few times since we moved in together twenty years ago, and I didn't want to face Jennifer this early.

Pulling onto Emory Road, I stopped at McDonald's for a coffee and steak and biscuit. I opened my coffee, intending to save the biscuit to eat at the office, and hit I-75 southbound. I was taking my first sip of scalding coffee when my cell phone began to play Scott Joplin's theme song from one of my favorite films, *The Sting*.

I read the name and answered, "Go ahead, John."

"Chief, have you been monitoring the radio this morning?" He sounded upset.

"No, John, I just left home. What's wrong?"

"Can you meet me at Trinity Chapel on Central Avenue Pike?"

"Sure, I'm on my way." John is a courageous man, a bit jittery at times, but something had obviously rattled him.

Three minutes later I arrived on scene. Trinity Chapel is a relatively small church, but fairly new with up swept architecture that made it seem to be rising higher than it really was, with perhaps the illusion of impending flight.

Two patrol units with lights flashing were there, one of which would be the first officer on the scene and the second probably there for securing the area. John's unmarked Chevrolet was behind the patrol units.

I saw John standing over a body, so I got out of my unit and walked to him. The expression on his face was terrible to see.

"John, you're an experienced Major Crimes detective, so I'm going to guess you know this victim."

"Chief, he's my pastor, who was going to preside at my wedding—and a close friend."

"John, do you want someone else to handle this case? I know it's hard when you are close to a victim."

"No, I'll pull myself together. I owe it to Bart to catch the coward who ambushed him." John swallowed hard, then almost visibly transformed into the expert investigator I knew him to be.

"A single round passed through his neck, just below his jawline. Judging by the massive exit wound, it's a large caliber, fired from some distance away," John said.

"We may never find the round because it was fired at an upward angle, maybe from that clump of trees a couple of hundred yards down the hill."

"That would have been a hell of a shot, John. Especially in subdued light. Maybe a trained sniper."

"There was no civilian report of the shot. Officer Malone, the first officer on the scene, found him and says he wasn't there an hour before when he rolled through doing property checks. So it was done in subdued light."

"How was it that Malone was here so soon after his last property check?" I asked.

"He picked up a sandwich at a deli down the road and brought it back here to eat, where the public wouldn't interrupt him."

"He seems to have lost his appetite, Chief. He's still fairly new at this."

"That was fortunate for us. Not all patrol officers are so conscientious. The body might have lain all night before anyone noticed," I said.

"That's my thought, Chief. I'll have the crime scene techs search the wooded area, but if he's a pro, there won't be a shell casing. And the round probably had enough velocity to have carried it for a mile or two, even after it was slowed by... Bart's neck."

"John, off the top of your head, do you know anyone who might have wanted to hurt the Reverend?"

"Chief, this an LGBT-friendly church in rural Knox County, and Bart was gay himself. We're always open game for some people."

"I know, John, but we'll catch this bastard. The department's resources are at your disposal. Consider your requests approved in advance. Do you want someone else to make family notifications?"

"No, Chief. I know his husband James and Bart's younger brother that he raised after their parents were killed in a car wreck. Bart and James were trying to adopt a baby."

"Whatever you require, John. I need to get downtown and brief the boss."

"Chief, this may not be the time to ask, but yesterday evening your secretary gave me an appointment for an interview for the open lieutenant's slot, and I didn't put in a bid."

"I put it in for you, John. I wanted to make sure the best candidates possible were interviewed. I *know* you don't want the responsibility. But I would appreciate it if you would do it for me. I won't force you to take the job, but I wish you would show up for the interview. Besides, you're about to become a married man and you need more regular hours."

"All right, Chief."

Sam was sitting behind his desk when I arrived at his office, sipping a cup of coffee. He glanced up at me as I entered.

"Well, I already have a good idea of what happened from listening to the radio and from the secretary's grapevine. Tell me what had John Freed so rattled this morning."

Sam was dressed in a dark blue suit and a pastel blue shirt, but he was not wearing a tie.

"Get a cup of coffee, and from your expression, you probably need to break out the cigarettes." He took the metal ashtray from his desk drawer as I poured my coffee and took a seat across from him.

"The victim is the Reverend Bart Wilson. John's pastor at Trinity Chapel. He was going to officiate at John's wedding."

"Hate crime, you think?"

"It's a possibility, but nothing left at the scene to indicate it," I replied.

I pushed my cigarettes and butane lighter across Sam's desk and we both lit up.

"I hope it isn't," Sam said, "though a lot of people are going to see it that way whether it is or not. The left-wingers because they expect it and the right-wingers because they'd like it to be true."

"You're right, Sam. I just hope we're able to wrap this up soon, but it looks like a sniper who knew what he was doing.

"No obvious clues and so far no shell casing, though the techs are searching as we speak, and the round that killed him exited and could be anywhere between the crime scene and the next county."

"It is what it is, then. I just got a list of candidates for the lieutenant's slot. I see John's name on it; do you want to postpone the interviews until we wrap this up?"

"No, let's do it. There's no guessing when this case will be solved, and if John gets the job, he can supervise the case and let somebody else do the grunt work."

"I take it you're leaning towards John?"

"I am, but I want to give all the applicants a fair shot at it."

"It's your bailiwick, Shy."

"All right, Sam. I expect to be here all day answering calls from the news media, old cops, and politicians looking for publicity."

"Don't tarry too long at work today, Shy. I understand you have some fence mending to do with a gorgeous Latina woman we both know."

"How in the hell did you..."

"I'm the Sheriff. Your Chief of Detectives reports to me. I know everything. And I know Jennifer. That's one Latina pot you don't want boiling too long."

I knew he was right and I wasn't looking forward to that conversation, not after sneaking out of the house before Jen was up.

EIGHT

The interview committee consisted of the Sheriff, Al Reagan, myself, and the Chief of Personnel, Lance Wittaker. Lance is what a fiction writer might call "a blade thin man" in his late forties. He has a soldier's posture and military haircut, and he served in Iraq during the Second Gulf War. He had also once been a near legendary street cop before unexpectedly transferring to supervisor of personnel.

We were gathered around the table in the conference room, finishing up our interview with Patrol Sergeant Larry Wilkin, our sixth and next-to-last candidate for the lieutenant's slot. The tall blond sergeant was impressive looking on paper and had carried himself well during the interview.

"Sergeant," Chief Whittaker said, "I see by what you've added under *outside activities* that you are active in your church. How important do you think this is overall in your life?"

"Sir, God, family, and love of country are what the United States was built on," the Sergeant replied.

It was a statement a lot of cops would have used to describe their lives—particularly military veterans.

"Good answer, Sergeant. That was my last question gentleman," Wittaker said.

"I think we have all the information we need, Sergeant. You're a veteran of the 82nd Airborne with two combat tours in Iraq during the Second Gulf War, and have a clean slate for the ten years you've been with this department. Do you have any questions for us?"

"Yes, Chief Tempest. Most of us know you served with distinction in the 173rd Airborne Brigade in Vietnam—but does a good military record really matter these days?"

"I can answer that, Sergeant," Sheriff Renfro said. "Not all of us served in the military, but it is one factor among many we'll consider when we choose a candidate.

"Chief Tempest, Chief of Detectives Reagan, and Chief Wittaker are all ex-military, but I'm not. I have, however, been a cop most of my adult life. We all take different paths to get where we're going. Does that answer your question?"

"I meant no offense, Sheriff," there was a pained look in the sergeant's eyes, "it was just curiosity. Nobody doubts *your* courage; it's legendary."

"No offense taken," Sam said. "Does anyone else have a question for the sergeant?"

"I have one question that comes to mind," Al said. "Sergeant, you are obviously a man of action, so will you be happy with a job that keeps you behind a desk a lot more than you're used to?"

"Chief, there are no unimportant jobs in this department. I'll do my best to utilize the skills I have to carry out my duties as a lieutenant if this committee chooses me."

"Good answer, Sergeant," Sam said. When the decision is made, you'll find an official letter in your box, informing you of the outcome. Thanks for your interest."

We waited as Sergeant Wilkin retrieved his dress hat and folder from the table and nodded to all of us as he left.

When he was gone, Al Reagan said, "You almost made the boy piss his pants, Sheriff—and he had it coming."

"God knows I admire military vets, but Wilkin needs to understand that balls-to-the-wall courage is not the *only* attribute of a good cop. Would you agree with that, Shiloh?"

Startled, I looked at my friend, trying to decide what he meant. Sam tended to think in layers.

"Of course there's more to the job than raw courage, Sam." He nodded, looking me in the eye. *What now?* I thought.

"All right, then, let's get our redheaded detective in here and wrap up this interview."

John Freed entered the room with the shyness of a virgin on a wedding night. It was hard to imagine him as an aggressive and passionate cop—except for those of us who had seen him in action.

"Have a seat, Detective," the Sheriff said. "Would you like some water or a soft drink?"

"Thanks, Sheriff. but I need to get this over with and get back to work on Bart Wilson's assassination."

"I haven't had a chance to offer my condolences for the loss of your friend, John—mainly because Chief Reagan says you've been working almost 24 hours a day for the week you've been on this case. Don't burn yourself out, John."

"Yes, sir," John said.

"John, you're here because your closest friends and supervisors believe you have skills beyond field work to offer the department," Sam said.

"Sheriff, I appreciate that, but I like the field work a lot more than a desk."

"Detective, do you think Al Reagan or Shiloh Tempest or I became supervisors because we didn't like the excitement of being in the field?"

"No, sir. You all were first rate cops before you became bosses," John said, looking the Sheriff in the eye for the first time.

"I had to harass them unmercifully in order to promote them because they both felt like you. Good cops love the streets. Let me ask you, John: What kind of bosses are they?"

"You're all still the same kind of cops I always admired," John said. "But you're *born* leaders. I'm not."

"Not so, John. We became leaders because leaders were needed. Three of these men you admire, myself included, think you're also a leader who shows up where he's needed without being asked and is willing to put his life on the line. That's *leadership*, John."

"But this case I'm working has to come first, Sheriff."

"Of course it does, John. But as a lieutenant, you can oversee the job and send investigators where *you* think they're needed—assuming you're deemed to be the best choice for the job," Sam said.

John nodded affirmatively.

"So you're willing to *consider* the job, John? We aren't going to force you to do it or think less of you if you don't," I said.

"I'll do whatever you all decide. But I still don't see myself as a supervisor," John said.

"In that case, Detective, do you have any questions for us?" the Sheriff asked.

"Yes, I do." John flushed just a bit and swallowed. "When can I get back to work on my case?"

"Consider your interview concluded," Sam Renfro said. "Hit the road and be careful."

After John left, we all looked at our notes and took a vote. John was rated number one by Sam, Al, and me.

Wittaker seemed to have been mightily impressed with Sergeant Wilkin, but the Chief of Personnel had voluntarily become an office pogue years earlier and was obviously out of touch with the streets. So we selected John as our new lieutenant.

NINE

The day went much as I had expected. Reporters called, trying to glean something I might accidentally let slip, as did the attorney general, who wanted enough information to call a press conference, because that's what he always does on high profile cases, especially with an election year coming up.

They were all disappointed, though, because I never let anything "slip" except on purpose when it suits my needs. But by three thirty I had endured all I could handle.

I told Holly I would be out of pocket for the rest of the day, unless something really important came up. She is very good at discerning what is important.

Besides, callers had to get past Sam's secretary before they got to me, and Madeline has been in the business longer than me or Sam. In fact, both of us are a little afraid of her.

On the way home, I stopped at a florist and bought Jennifer a dozen yellow carnations, because she prefers carnations over roses.

I made another stop at the supermarket to put together a simple but elegant-by-my-standards meal.

It had been a while since I had gone home early to cook, and I definitely needed to warm up the chill that had been between us since the morning when I had skulked out of the house to avoid talking to her.

As I wheeled into the driveway, Magdala's head and feet appeared in the kitchen window. I don't know how dogs experience time, but our German shepherd knows when a schedule changes.

By the time I took out my keys, Magdala was sniffing under the kitchen door like a vacuum cleaner and whimpering for me to hurry—even before she smelled the pork tenderloin in the grocery bag I was carrying as I put it on the counter beside the door.

"How's my baby girl?" I grabbed her by the head and massaged her ears. She groaned with pleasure, all the while eyeing the grocery bag.

"You're not at all subtle are you, girl? Come on, let's go outside."

She glanced one more time at the grocery bag, then dashed outside. I followed and watched her check the perimeter of her domain to see what creature might have visited since her last security check.

Finally, she found the perfect spot and relieved herself, then raced back, no doubt still thinking of the delightful odor coming from the grocery bag.

Back in the kitchen, I opened the bag and removed a pack of Pup-peroni sticks for dogs, tore the top off that bag, and handed a treat to Magdala.

She sniffed the treat, then looked at me as if to say, "So you're keeping the good stuff and giving me a dry stick of meat?"

She didn't hesitate long, though, and was soon lying by the kitchen table, nibbling on her treat as I put the meat and corn on the cob in the refrigerator.

When I started back to the bedroom to change into my moccasins, jeans, and a black tee shirt, Magdala sighed deeply, glanced at the refrigerator, then followed me down the hall.

As I changed into my casual clothes, I caught a glance of myself in the full-length mirror on the wall.

I saw a short stocky man with dark, closely-cropped hair that seemed to have more silver in it every day. Still reasonably athletic looking for my age, though.

I had sliced the pork tenderloin into medallions, taken the fresh corn off the cob, and was making a batter for small cornbread pancakes that are a favorite of mine and Jennifer's, when John called me.

"Yes, Detective Freed, how may I help you?"

"A patrol officer stopped Todd Aiken and filled out an interview card the night Bart Wilson was killed and he was only five miles from the church an hour before the shooting. I want to pull him in and grill him." A field interview card is filled out by patrol officers who stop someone they find of interest but have nothing to arrest or cite him for.

"John, first of all, we don't have any reason to suspect that Aiken even knew your pastor. And what address did he give for the field interview card?"

"He's living at that fleabag rooming house on Clinton Highway that used to be a motel, the one where Jerry Carpenter was living when he was killed. I distinctly remember that Aiken lived in West Knoxville when he first was interviewed after he became a murder suspect."

"John, he just got out of the funny farm and he's probably in the best place he can afford. Why was he stopped in the first place?"

"The officer saw him pulling out of the rooming house and recognized him as someone who hadn't been there before," John said with a sigh. I could almost picture John's face sadden.

"So he lives in the neighborhood where an alert patrol officer spotted him as being out of place?"

"You're right, Chief. No valid reason to bring him in, and if he is stalking you, we wouldn't want to tip him off that we suspect him."

"John, go home and rest. I can make that an order if you like."

"That won't be necessary, Chief. I've been turning over rocks too long this week and I need to rest."

"You never know which rock the killer will be under, John, but you can't turn them all over in a week."

"All right, I'm on my way home," the weary detective said.

As I returned to my work space, I noticed that Magdala was looking at the spot where I had placed the sliced pork tenderloin, sniffing the air.

"My dogs don't eat raw meat, Magdala. You may as well lie down and relax." She all but collapsed with a deep sigh, giving me a remarkably petulant glare, and was still lying sadly by the table when Jennifer came home a few minutes later.

"Something smells really good," Jennifer said as she entered the kitchen. "Settle down, Magdala! What's she whining about?"

Our German shepherd was putting on quite a show. "She's trying to tell you how badly I've treated her because I would not give her any raw tenderloin."

"You may as well settle down, Magdala. You know we don't feed you raw meat. You can have a taste when it's cooked."

Magdala stared in disbelief that Jennifer had refused to take her side of the dispute. She once more collapsed on the floor and stared at both of us in a forlorn manner.

"You haven't cooked for us in a while," Jennifer said. Then spotting the fresh carnations I had put in a vase on the table, her eyes opened widely. "And flowers for *me*?"

"Yes, but let Magdala think they're for her also, or she may have a nervous breakdown."

"We got flowers *and* a home cooked meal, Magdala," my beautiful *compañera* said. Our German shepherd sighed again, obviously not impressed.

"It's an apology gesture, my love. I know I've behaved badly lately."

"Honestly, Shiloh, for a man with such a mastery of language, why don't you just say how you *feel*? Not that I don't appreciate the extras."

"I was raised in a household where emotions were kept concealed, no matter what."

I transferred the creamed corn I had made from the fresh corn right off the cob, along with the tenderloin medallions and stack of cornbread pancakes to serving dishes and put them on the table.

"I know, my little Rooster. I know." She opened her purse that she had put on the counter when Magdala besieged her, and removed a small box. "I also made a heartwarming purchase today, but we eat before I give it to you."

And we did.

"Wonderful, *mi amor*." Jennifer pushed her dish away and took a sip of coffee. "Very good. Is this a new blend?"

"Yes, Ethiopian blend. We hadn't tried a new coffee lately, so I picked it up today. Shall we give Magdala a piece of tenderloin? She's drooling."

"By all means, give Magdala a slice of tenderloin, but save me enough for a sandwich tomorrow."

Magdala was suddenly at my side, nose quivering. She took the tenderloin from my hand and swallowed it in one bite.

"Here you go, Soldier," Jennifer said, handing me the small box from her purse.

"Is it a ring?" I asked. "Or a new ear stud, though I haven't worn one of those in years."

"Just open it, silly man."

I opened it and saw a Vietnam era Zippo cigarette lighter engraved with the words: "Fort Jackson, South Carolina, Infantry."

"I'm stunned, Jen. I bought one just like this when I was in basic training and lost it fifteen years ago. I think it was two dollars, including engraving." I opened it and turned the wheel and it lit the first time, as promised.

"That *may* be the one you lost. I found it in a little curio and antique shop in the Old City. The young woman who sold it to me said they sent it back to the factory for refurbishing. And by the way, don't ask how much the price has gone up since you first purchased it."

"It cost you a pretty penny, I'm sure." I leaned over and kissed her.

"I think cleanup can wait a while," Jennifer said. "Last one naked has to *do* the cleanup."

She began to shed her clothes as she headed for the bedroom. She still looks like Madeline Stowe from behind.

The only other scene I remember from that film is Emilio Estevez telling Richard Dreyfus how disgusting it was when he ate a sandwich made with a runny egg over easy.

TEN

I was sitting in the recreation room, kicked back in my recliner with my computer in my lap and a cup of coffee on the table beside me, when Jennifer came in carrying a stack of papers and folders and a cup of coffee.

She sat down in her matching recliner, put her coffee on the little table beside her chair, and began sorting through papers and folders.

"What are you up to, Chiquita? I asked.

"*Chiquita?* Do I look tiny to you or like a little woman?"

"Not really. Just taking advantage of being one of the few men I know with the nerve to call you by a diminutive nickname." I replied. "You're just the right size."

"All right then, I'll let it slide. I have a couple of things to go over with you about John's wedding, but first I have a question that's been nagging at me."

"I'm all ears, *Niña.*"

"Are you trying to annoy me? I'm aware that you have picked up a pitifully few words of Spanish in the last twenty years."

"All right, I'll be *good* instead of *playful*. What's the question?"

"Did you actually use *gardyloo* to warn a cop in your new novel 'to duck or be shot?'"

"You looked it up, didn't you?" I asked.

"Yes I did. It stuck in my mind. Did you actually use it?"

"Naw, I was just messing with Freddy."

"That's what I thought. All right then, about John's wedding. He wants you to be his best man and is afraid to ask you."

"I thought he'd ask Al Reagan."

"No, Al is going to be CJ's best man."

"The world is changing, Jen. I'll be glad to serve as John's best man," I answered. "And while we're on the subject, what will the attire be?"

"Casual. You won't have to wear a tux or even a tie."

"That's good."

"Do you want to go over the cost for flowers and food?" Jen asked.

"No, it would just make me nervous."

"So, a bottomless budget?"

"Now you're messing with me."

"Yes I am," she said, flashing dimples.

"Planning the wedding has gotten John's mind off the death of his friend and pastor," I said, "I was afraid he was going to work himself into a psychotic break."

"Has there been any progress at all, Shiloh?"

"Yes. To our amazement, the sniper left behind a shell casing, probably because it was so dark in the woods and he was in a hurry. There were no prints. It could have come from any rifle from the Russian AK-47 to the American M-14. We hope the state crime lab will be able to narrow it down some, but we're not holding our breath."

Al Reagan, John Freed, and I gathered in my office to discuss the Reverend Bart Wilson murder.

"Does everyone have coffee or a soft drink?" I asked.

Reagan nodded affirmatively and Freed raised a can of diet soda.

"One of you catch me up on the latest information," I said, as I got Reagan's coffee.

"Shy, the state crime lab says the most likely rifle used in the assassination was an M-14 rifle. But the identification won't hold up in court based on the shell casing alone.

"It's a hit or miss deal based in a large part on looking at tool marks on casings they've collected and the expertise of the technician doing the check."

"Well, that's something, a starting place, Al," I said.

"I think they stopped manufacturing the M-14 around 1964, but modifications on the M-14 rifles went on for 20 years, and that's not counting modifications made by individuals. Over all, approximately 1.3 million were manufactured."

Reagan stopped and took a sip of coffee, and I said, "I also read that the original M-14 sniper rifle came with a wooden stock, but was later changed to fiberglass in the sniper edition. So as of now, I guess we'll be on the lookout for *any* M-14 rifle. Not a lot to go on."

"You're right, Al, it's not much," I said, "but we've started with less evidence. Anything else pertaining to the case?"

Both men indicated by their expressions that there was nothing else. John was sipping his diet drink and Al was polishing the lens of his wire-rimmed glasses.

"In that case, John, I'll be glad to serve as your best man—assuming it's really all right with Al. "

"We talked it out, Shy. I'm honored to be CJ's best man," Al said. "Jennifer was going through plans for flowers, refreshments, and a photographer, and she needs to touch base again with you, John."

"Gosh, Chief, it will be my honor," John said.

"Don't get mushy, John. Jen's doing all the work and enjoying it. But I have a question: Do you really want to serve catered barbecue? We can spring for something a little more elegant."

"Chief, most of the guests will be cops and their family members. Nobody will expect lobster and caviar," John said, flushing just a bit.

"Good point, John." I said, "Anything else should be taken up with the lovely Jennifer. And if there's nothing else, we can all get back to work."

"You busy, Bubba?" Sheriff Renfro asked from my doorway.

"Nope. Just turning the sniper case over in my mind, trying to puzzle out whether we've overlooked something."

"Then I think we need to talk." He entered my office, closing the door behind him, grabbed a chair and straddled it like a horse, facing me. "This may require a smoke."

"By all means," I said putting an ashtray on my desk and sliding a pack of filtered Camels and my newly acquired lighter to him.

"Nice," he said, "you've moved up from those cheap disposable lighters." He lit his cigarette and passed the pack and lighter back to me.

"Actually, I'm just going back to the lighter I lost years ago. Jen found this one in a curio shop and bought it for me."

"Someday we're going to talk about how you ended up with a woman like Jennifer and I didn't. But not today."

"Okay boss, hit me with it." I had been waiting to hear from Sam about whatever was bothering him. We had been friends too long to not notice when things were out of kilter with either of us.

"I'm going to flood the area of your house with a dozen extra unmarked units from the retired unmarked-units fleet on the day of John's wedding, and I thought I'd let you know in advance."

"Oh?" It wasn't what I had been expecting, so I lit a cigarette and waited for Sam to continue.

"We don't know whether the killing of John's pastor was a hate crime, but I'm not willing to discount it yet."

"That had crossed my mind, Sam. Sounds like a good idea to me. If it was a homophobic hate shooting, a gay wedding would be the perfect time and place for the shooter to make another public statement."

"Right. I don't think we ought to get caught unprepared. I knew you'd notice the old unmarked units so I wanted to give you notice."

"I appreciate that, Sam."

"Now we need to discuss what you were expecting," Sam said.

"Go ahead. I think I'll have another cigarette. You want one?"

"No. I don't think it's a two-cigarette problem—yet. But when I hear from people who love you, know you, and respect you as well as anyone on Earth, that you've been behaving in a *peculiar* manner, I pay attention."

I lit another cigarette, took a deep drag, and released it.

"You know, Sam, sometimes I think I don't have a private life. My friends plot against me with my doctor and my wife and my boss, and for all I know my priest. Everyone has off days!"

"*Plot*? If that's what you really believe, we may have a bigger problem than I thought—and I didn't know you had a priest."

"No, no! I'm not *paranoid* and the priest is a friend of mine. I'm going to surprise John. She has agreed to do his wedding."

"*She*? A female priest?"

"She's an *Episcopal* priest, Sam. They have a ceremony for same sex couples. I met her on a case I was working and we hit it off."

"All right, no big deal. Tell me about the fast food assistant manager you terrorized," Sam said.

"I didn't t*errorize* him, Sam—just taught him something about courtesy!"

"Come on, Shy, you're perfectly capable of *terrorizing* a suspect. In fact you're good at it. But I never saw you do it unless you were dealing with really *bad* people, not just run of the mill idiots."

"I just lost it for a few seconds, Sam. I didn't kill anybody."

"All right, I'll concede that everyone has a bad moment every now and then, but you're one of the steadiest men I ever worked with. Especially under pressure. Are you sure there's not something you need to get off your chest?"

"Are you also going to talk to me about the horrid way I've been treating my agent and editor?"

"No, I was going to skip that, since I couldn't bring it up without fingering Jennifer. But since you brought it up, are the two things related?" Sam asked.

"Maybe, Sam, maybe. Do you ever have moments when you think you've experienced everything there is, and you're just waiting for the next shoe to drop?"

"Yes I have and I'd guess we all have those moments like that—but not to the point that we change the beneficiaries on our life insurance and retirement funds."

"All right, Sam. Now I *am* pissed! My beneficiary is *my* business. And just *how* did you find this out?"

"Settle down, Shy! I'm the Sheriff of this county and I make it my business to know everything that happens—especially when it's happening to my best friend and chief deputy!"

Both of us had reached the "voices raised point." I decided to dial it back a couple of notches, so I took a deep breath before I spoke again and said something I would definitely regret.

"What do you want, Sam? Do you think I need to have a new psychological exam? If that's what you want, you're the boss—but it's not a good time to be off the playing field for me."

"I agree, but your welfare is *my* responsibility. I've heard you say, 'Who will watch the watchers?'"

"Yeah, it's a variation of the Roman poet Juvenal's *Quis custodiet ipsos custodes?* 'Who will guard the guardians?' I didn't know you ever listened to me."

"Hey, I happen to have a Master's degree. It's in Criminal Justice, but I actually had to attend classes in sociology and psychology and I took Latin as an elective.

"The people at the bottom of the food chain have to depend on the people taking care of them. And that's *us* Shy."

"Point taken. Just out of curiosity, was it Freed or Reagan who expressed concerns?"

"They both told me you're talking like Wyatt Earp and don't seem concerned with your own safety?"

"Do I have no secrets, Sam?"

"Not from *me,*" he said.

ELEVEN

The weather was beautiful for John and CJ's wedding, except for people with pollen allergies. The East Tennessee pollen count for grass and trees is almost always high, except right after heavy rain or during a hard freeze.

The week leading up to the wedding had been fairly quiet, even in the police business. Domestic disturbances continued, burglaries went on unabated, and there was no progress in the murder of John's pastor.

And of course, John received his lieutenant's bars in a private ceremony in the Sheriff's office.

The Reverend Ella Fritz, who had agreed to preside at the wedding, was mingling in our large backyard with other guests, wearing her traditional black shirt and clerical collar. She was a sturdy but shapely woman in her early forties.

I had taken John and Ella to lunch a few days before the wedding and they hit it off immediately.

Buddy's BBQ, a popular local restaurant and catering chain, had set up a table where they would serve not only barbecued pork and chicken, but also baked beans, green beans, coleslaw, and potato salad. It was pretty much what is called "country cooking" in East Tennessee.

The crowd was relatively small, with 30 invited guests and their spouses or partners, mostly personal friends.

It had been decided that all invitations would be delivered personally, without written invitations. John and CJ had decided this themselves because they knew to some it would arouse angry and perhaps violent feelings.

Cops, for the most part, had been remarkably tolerant of gay officers. There had been more or less *openly* gay cops in their ranks since the late seventies. It just wasn't mentioned. In some cases, this has remained true.

"Well, Hoss, this looks like a hippie bash from the seventies. Where did you find those old plastic lantern covers and who picked the music from the sixties and seventies the disc jockey's playing?"

Sam Renfro had entered through the house and made his way to the back deck where I stood watching the crowd.

"John and CJ found the lantern covers somewhere and they picked the music. Who would have suspected that John was a retro kind of guy?"

"Yeah, those baby blue tuxes the two of them are wearing probably were in style at *your* high school prom."

"Those will be the only tuxedos here today, and I'm not that old, Sam." I took out my cigarettes and lit one, then extended the pack to Sam.

"You're the last Vietnam vet in the department—and I'll pass on the cigarette. A sheriff shouldn't be seen smoking in public."

"I lied about my age to get in the Army, Sam. Most Vietnam vets *are* older than I am."

"Don't be so touchy, Shy. I already know you're twenty years older than that beautiful companion of yours, but I'll keep your secret."

"Speaking of Jennifer, she just waved me down. They must be ready to start. They'll need me and Al in place to walk behind John and CJ."

"I see you're wearing a tie and jacket." Sam said.

"And a pastel shirt because Jen threatened to burn my plaid shirts if I didn't. But I'd point out that my jacket came off the rack, and won't outshine John's and CJ's tuxes. Nothing like that tailored blue suit and imported silk tie you're sporting, Sam."

"The Sheriff is expected to shine, Shiloh, because my second job title is *politician*."

Below, the wedding guests took their seats in white folding chairs loaned to us by John's church, Trinity Chapel.

The Reverend Ella Fritz took her place before the congregation, wearing a stole and chasuble, which is like a poncho that fits over the inner garments, with the color depending on the liturgical season. She could have dressed less formally, but had chosen not to do so.

John and CJ were both obviously nervous as Al and I took our places beside them. Then, as the DJ put on the wedding march, we took our walk between the guests and paused before Ella. Al and I stepped back.

A hymn was sung, and I'm certain things were said that I didn't understand and don't remember, not having a Catholic background, but I remember the opening and closing because they were very similar to other marriages I had witnessed that were *not* same sex unions.

"Dearly Beloved: We have come together in the presence of God to witness and bless the joining together of John Walter Freed and Charles Jonathon Mayhew in holy matrimony..." Ella's voice was steady and somehow reassuring.

John and CJ were obviously nervous. But they were two fine looking men. CJ, blond, and husky and John, with red hair and alabaster skin that some women would kill for, stood like soldiers at attention.

Soon the words coming from the Reverend Fritz receded into the background as my eyes began to wander, looking for something out of place and potential threats, traits cut into my soul by years of habit.

Our subdivision sits on a ridge that would be called a small mountain anywhere but Appalachia.

Behind Ella Fritz was our half acre yard, surrounded by a five feet high chain link fence. Beyond the fence was undeveloped land even higher than our subdivision and thickly wooded. Across from the front of our home was a similar area behind the houses across the street.

Most people would have found the area restful and pleasant, but I knew that to the eight or ten cops attending the wedding the wooded areas surrounding the subdivision would be perceived as places where concealed assassins could be lurking—and not because we were at a same sex marriage, but because good cops know that violence can be hiding anywhere.

The crowd moved almost imperceptibly and my attention snapped back to the wedding in progress. I focused on the priest's words, and realized that John and CJ were married.

"Will all of you witnessing these promises do all in your power to uphold these two persons in their marriage?" Ella asked.

The gathered Episcopalians and Catholics present responded with, "We will."

John and CJ turned slightly towards each other smiling, and at the same moment the yellow lantern cover and the light bulb inside it just above the priest's head exploded, and a microsecond later one of the officers in the congregation recognized the crack of the gunshot and yelled, "Get down!"

Pandemonium broke out as officers in the crowd pushed their spouses to the ground and everyone dived for cover. From the corner of my eye I saw the portable table from Buddy's BBQ that held potato chips and cellophane wrapped dessert cakes turn over. For a split second, I thought the steam table containing gallons of scalding water and hot barbecue and vegetables was also going to turn over onto quests who had taken cover on the ground, but it only wobbled and settled back down.

Thank God for small favors.

"This is Unit One," I heard Sam say into his portable radio, "shots fired! No one hit that I can see. All units converge on the area of Unit Two's residence and stop any vehicle moving in close proximity!"

As the guests picked themselves up, Sam appeared beside me. "Give me your take, Shiloh."

"The shooter hit what he was aiming at; it was a high-powered round that we'll never find judging by the crack of the round. So it's probably the same shooter who killed John's pastor."

"I believe you're right. This one was a statement about the wedding."

"Special Detail Seven to Unit One," Sam's radio crackled.

"Unit One, go ahead."

"Unit One, could you and Unit Two see us on Cedar Hill. We have a suspect in custody."

"Ten-four," Sam said, "we'll be on our way momentarily."

"Sheriff, I'll ride with you and Shiloh. Whoever the sonofabitch is, I want to be there!"

We had not realized that John was close enough to overhear what had been said. His normal neatly combed hair was disheveled and his pale face was mottled, which happens when you dive for cover, trying to protect a loved one.

"No, Lieutenant," Sam said. "You just got married and I haven't given you my present. You and CJ are going to Gatlinburg on me." Sam reached into his inner jacket pocket, removed an envelope, and handed it to the tall redheaded newly promoted lieutenant.

"But, Sheriff..." John began.

"John, this is one of the finest hotels in Gatlinburg. For at least two days you and your new husband are going to live the high life, including room service and the liquor bar on me.

"If you show up here before at least two days are over, I am going to take it as a personal affront. Now, mingle with your guests, some of whom I know have more loot for the two of you. Your case will be in competent hands until you get back."

"Sheriff... this is an expensive gift," John said.

"I can afford it," Sam said. "Now get back to your wedding party. Don't let this bastard ruin your day. Shiloh and I will see who they have. When your guests leave, you go to Gatlinburg and stay off the clock."

"All right, Sheriff, this is a wonderful gift," John said. "And, Chief, you know how much I appreciate what you've done..."

"Bye, John. We'll see you in two days. Let's roll Sheriff," I said. John watched as we ran to Sam's car, shoulders down, but resigned.

The location to which we had been called was five minutes away on a road that ran parallel to the subdivision in which my house is located.

We arrived to find two uniformed officers standing by one of the retired unmarked units Sam had put in the neighborhood. Sitting in the back seat was Todd Aiken.

"Who is that in the car, Shiloh? Do you recognize him?" Sam asked.

"That is Todd Aiken, the man who tried to kill me twice, Sam."

"Maybe this is going to be an open and shut case," the Sheriff said as we exited the cruiser.

One of the patrol officers, a stocky young man of medium height, was at the front of Sam's car. I saw that his name tag said Larry Neff.

"Fill us in," Sam said. "Did you catch him coming out of the woods?"

"No, Sheriff, he was standing beside his car and flagged us down when he saw the blue light in the dash. He says he saw the shooter and he was driving one of our unmarked units. Described him as tall, thin, and wearing a hooded brown jacket."

I walked around and opened the cruiser door where Aiken was sitting. As usual his hair was neatly trimmed, soldier like.

"Todd. Why were you here?"

"Chief, I'm trying to redeem myself for what I did to you. I was on the lookout for snipers because I knew about the wedding."

"How could you have possibly known about the wedding? It was never officially announced."

"Chief Tempest, I don't mean to be a smart ass, but your officers talk a lot when they're on their lunch breaks.

"I was sitting behind two of them at the Waffle House on Emory a few days ago. One was kind of cool with the wedding, but the other one was pretty hostile to the idea and said he didn't think you and the Sheriff should be involved in a gay wedding.

"I got enough details from listening to them that I decided to *unofficially* help out. I have my crazy times when I go off my meds, but I was an Army Ranger and figured out the best places for a sniper to set up.

"I rolled up on this guy coming out of the woods with a rifle. He jumped in one of them old unmarked cars. Do you believe me?"

"That's what he told us, Chief." Officer Neff said. "He wasn't armed and he waved us down."

"Sounds preposterous to me," Sam said. "What do you think, Shiloh?"

"We knew he was living fairly close by. He *was* a Ranger and he wouldn't have been caught if he didn't want to be. I suggest we put crime scene technicians in the area where Aiken said the shooter came out.

"What can you tell us about the shooter besides that he was tall and thin, wearing a hooded jacket, Todd?"

"I'm pretty sure his weapon was an M-14 sniper rifle."

"*What?*" I stared at Todd Aiken hard. "How could you possibly know what kind of rifle it was from this distance?"

"Chief, rifles have profiles, like the side view of a person. I trained with an M-14 sniper rifle and a dozen others. I didn't have to be close to tell what kind it was. I saw the *profile*."

I remembered stories from my time in Vietnam that when our military first changed to M-16s from M-14s, a lot of soldiers and Marines didn't like the light weight ammo used by the M-16s, so they picked up AK-47s because there was a lot of ammo available and started using them.

I heard there were instances where other Americans in low light situations saw the silhouette of the Russian made rifles and fired on them. It made sense what Aiken had said. Weapons do have profiles and a sniper would know them.

"Shiloh, should we put out a BOLO on the shooter's vehicle?" Sam asked.

"You're the sheriff, but if we BOLO a vehicle description, it will tip off the real shooter, because he *has* to be one of us."

"You're right," Sam said. "I'll get the technicians out here and check to see if we were missing an extra retired vehicle today from the service center. You go back and see if you can salvage at least part of John's and CJ's wedding."

"Chief, does this mean I can go?" Todd Aiken asked.

"Todd, you stay here with these officers and give them a statement. When the crime scene techs get here, they'll test you and your car for gunshot residue. If it comes up negative, you can leave."

"It will, Chief. I was just trying to redeem myself."

"And I appreciate it, Todd, but your work on the case is finished. Your prowling around can only complicate things, especially if you run into John Freed while he's working. *Understand?*" He nodded affirmatively.

"And Todd, consider yourself on your way to being *redeemed*."

He smiled like a child on Christmas morning.

TWELVE

Jennifer and I put the last of our dirty dinnerware in the dishwasher as Magdala followed us around, hoping for leftovers. But there hadn't been any leftovers because cops and their families spring back pretty quickly, especially where free food is involved.

There's an old cop joke that says a police officer who turns down free food or coffee can be booted out of the Fraternal Order of Police.

"So, fill me in. It's been frantic around here and I knew you didn't want to discuss the case in front of other people. I saw you talking on your cell phone off and on all day."

"Part of it you probably have already figured out. I know the officers present were following the action on their portables," I said.

"Cops are never far from their radios and weapons," Jennifer said. She had pulled her long, dark hair back in a ponytail.

"Sam had assigned a dozen officers to prowl the area in old, retired unmarked cruisers. *Thirteen* had actually left the service center. But the extra one was taken and returned without anyone noticing.

"There's a lot of traffic in and out of there during the day. We do know which vehicle was *not* assigned to the special detail. Sam had it towed in for crime scene techs to see if the driver, who is undoubtedly also the shooter, left any traces."

"He's a bold *asno* to have taken an old cruiser in broad daylight," Jennifer said, angrily.

"He could have picked it up the night before, when there was only one attendant there. Everybody knows that old man naps a lot, and there's nobody else watching when he takes a bathroom break. Did you just say *asshole* in Spanish?"

"More like dumb-ass or *jackass*, definitely a term of derision. Asshole is such a *crude* term," she replied. "Go ahead."

"That's pretty much it. If whoever took the car and returned it without being spotted, is a supervisor with a key to the lot, we may not identify him."

"How did they know about the wedding and the location, Shiloh? We didn't make a formal announcement."

"The *grapevine*, Jen. Plus. Cops are blabbermouths when they don't know civilians are listening. That's how Todd Aiken found out."

Oops, the name had slipped out.

"Todd Aiken! The man who tried to kill you twice? He was in the woods above our home, and you didn't think it was important enough to tell me before now?"

"I was going to tell you, but I was waiting for things to calm down a bit. Todd is the one who gave us the tip. And he wasn't in the woods."

"Why was he there at all? Did you *macho* men think I was too weak to be brought in on a threat to your life?"

"Todd was trying to *redeem* himself for what he tried to do to me. You know how I feel about that, Jen."

"Yes, but you believe *everyone* is capable of redemption. Not *everybody* is, *mi amor!*"

"I'm sorry, Jen. We've had Todd under surveillance since they released him from the hospital. I should have told you, but…"

"But you didn't want me to worry. Protect the *little woman*, right?"

Jennifer got up from the couch and stalked off to the bedroom. Magdala looked at me, whimpered, and followed my compañera to the bedroom. My dog loves me, but she seldom crosses Jennifer.

"Chief, no offense, but you look terrible," Holly Sowers said. "Let me get you a cup of coffee. I *know* you don't like being waited on, but you need coffee before you try to shave. A few weeks ago, I put a disposable razor and can of shaving cream in your medicine cabinet, and you have a fresh shirt hanging in your restroom."

She stood waiting, a petite young woman, perhaps twenty-three or twenty-four. Blonde with a wholesome look—the kind of woman a man might describe as *cute* if that man had no sense of how to address independent young females in the twenty-first century.

"Thank you, Holly." I sat down at my desk and took a sip of the coffee Holly had put in front of me. It was black and had the artificial sweetener the doctor had recently put me on.

I had tiptoed into our bedroom in the slacks I had slept in without waking Jennifer, got my pistol and holster, keys and wallet, then grabbed the shirt and jacket I had worn the day before to keep from opening the squeaky closet door.

Magdala had followed me into the kitchen and I let her out to relieve herself, dressed in the kitchen, and let our German shepherd back in the house. She whimpered in protest at the change in routine as I quietly left.

"Chief," Holly said from the door, "Tom Abernathy from Knoxville P D is asking to see you."

"Sure, send him in," I said, wondering why Tom was out at such an early hour.

He nodded as he came in. "Chief."

"You're out awfully early, Tom."

"And you look like a man who slept on the couch last night," Tom said.

"Let's not get into that. I know you're not here this early just for a cup of coffee, though Holly does brew a good cup of coffee."

"I've been overseeing the criminal intelligence squad," Abernathy said. "One of my guys managed to infiltrate this little coven of supposedly Christian zealots we think may have been involved in some vandalism cases at gay bars. He recorded a sermon, and since I've been following your case in the newspapers I thought you might be interested.

"I put the recording on a thumb drive so you could see it before my boss sees it and feeds it to the news media to make your agency look bad."

Tom handed me the thumb drive and I opened my laptop, preparing to watch the video.

"When did you start working criminal intelligence, Tom?"

"I don't *work* it. That would be the fun part and Chief Frank Hodge isn't going to allow that. He's still pissed because you and I uncovered his love nest and used it to make him act more *reasonable* when your friend Jerry Carpenter was murdered at the Sunsphere.

"Mostly, I coordinate data from narcotics, criminal intelligence and criminal investigations, and put it in a summary that Hodge's feeble mind can understand."

"Sounds like a waste of investigative talent," I said, plugging the thumb drive into my laptop.

"That has never bothered Hodge where I'm concerned. I'd say he's a racial bigot but he's nasty to everyone."

I leaned forward, taking a sip of coffee, to look at the video that had popped up on the screen. It was a man behind a pulpit and there was a large wooden cross on the wall behind him.

"Is this a storefront church?" I asked.

"Whether or not it's a *church* is debatable. It used to be a shoe store in an old block building. They call it the Sanctified Gospel Temple, but you'll see—or hear—for yourself whether you think it's actually a *Christian* church."

The man behind the pulpit, dressed in a white shirt and no tie, like the Baptist preachers in little country churches I attended as a child, opened his Bible and began to read.

"'If a man also lie with mankind, as he lieth with a woman, both of them have committed an abomination: they shall surely be put to death; their blood shall be upon them.' Reading from God's *only* Bible, the King James Version.'"

"He's definitely not a scholar if he's still pushing that old 'god only wrote one bible nonsense,'" I said.

"Does he look familiar to you, Chief?"

"Well, the video isn't very clear and my eyes aren't what they used to be," I said.

"The Bible called it an *abomination*," the preacher continued, "but we need to call the practitioners of same sex relations what they are—a disgusting, vile perversion of God's Holy Word! *A perversion worthy of death."*

"It didn't take him long to make his point," I said.

"Does he maybe *sound* familiar, Shy?"

"He sounds like every other self-taught Bible-thumping moron I ever heard before, Tom." But I clicked for a full screen look at the video and turned up the volume.

I put my face closer to the screen and squinted.

"And I can tell you brothers and sisters," the preacher's voice was louder, "we ought to be arresting these disgusting queers and *executing* them, instead of allowing them to come into our homes through television!"

"I am here to tell you that God, family, and love of country are what the United States was built on—and these faggots are taking over everything. They can't *reproduce* so they have to *seduce* our daughters and sons!"

When I heard the words, *"God, family, and love of country are what the United States was built on,"* there was suddenly bile in the back of my throat. I knew exactly where I had last heard those words.

"Oh my God!" I said, and leaned back in my chair.

"The undercover guy we finally got into the Sanctified Gospel Temple went in with a homeless guy he had been cultivating.

"The preacher and he had worked a joint operation together at one time, but the preacher didn't recognize him with a beard and long hair."

"Watch closely. We're to the point where our guy gets up to use the bathroom and pans the crowd."

I leaned closer to the screen, while pushing the intercom button. "Holly, is the Sheriff here?"

"Yes he is, I just saw him go into his office, Chief."

"Tell his secretary I need him in my office as soon as possible!"

"I don't think Madeline's here yet, but I'll go get him, Chief."

"Tom, can you start this video to the opening?"

"You're almost to the group shot, Shy. You might see someone else you know."

"This tape will be examined in *minute* detail by our technical people, but I want Sam to see the beginning. We interviewed that sonofabitch for a lieutenant's job a few days ago!"

THIRTEEN

Sam Renfro entered my office through the public door, which had to be electronically opened by my secretary.

He was wearing a tailored gray suit and two-tone maroon and gray saddle oxfords. When I had tried to rag him about the shoes when he first got them, he had responded by telling me that only a *secure* man with *cajones* the size of basketballs would have the nerve to wear such shoes.

"Nice to see you, Tom Abernathy. You here to apply for a job?" Sam said.

Then, not waiting for Abernathy to respond, Sam said, "Shy, I hope you've got coffee for me at this ungodly hour. Madeline's late for the first time since she took over the job of managing my time."

"Right there on the front of my desk, in the black and gold cup that says *Top Cop*."

"*Wow*! Top Cop. When did you buy that one for me?" Sam asked, pulling up a chair and straddling it backwards like a horse.

"I didn't. Al Reagan and John Freed bought it for me when we worked our first case together."

"I'd be hurt if I didn't remember that case so well. It's the one that brought you back to us, Shy."

Sam took a sip of his coffee, then asked, "Will this be a one or two cigarette crisis. I'd say maybe two from the expressions you and Tom are wearing."

I took the old metal ashtray from my desk drawer and slid my cigarettes and lighter across the desk to Sam. He lit up, took a drag, and said, "You don't smoke do you, Tom? I don't either except when my Chief Deputy is about to toss me a hot potato."

Abernathy shook his head to indicate he was still a non-smoker, and Sam slid my cigarettes and lighter back across the desk. I pushed the play button and turned the laptop computer around so Sam could see the full screen, then lit a cigarette.

"A video. Don't tell me one of my deputies has an excessive force complaint,"

"If only it was. Look closely and listen to the voice, Sam." I said.

The Sheriff leaned in closer and listened intently. When the phrase that had made me recognize the preacher was uttered, Sam said, "*Sonofabitch*, Sergeant Wilkin! It appears he really is active in his church and does believe in *God, family, and love of country*. Just not the same God most of us believe in."

"Shiloh, get with Al Reagan and catch him up. And if you will, see if Jen can come in before lunch. I want a sharp legal mind outside this department so that word doesn't leak out.

"Abernathy, can you get your undercover guy in here quietly without getting yourself in trouble with your boss?"

"I can do that, Sheriff. About eleven this morning all right?" Abernathy asked.

"That will be good. I'm going to walk this recording down to my personal computer guy and have it analyzed and enhanced as much as possible."

"Sam, it would probably be better if you asked Jen for a favor." I said. He turned and stared at me.

"What have you done to that long-suffering woman now, Shiloh?"

"I accidentally let Todd Aiken's name slip last night. She didn't know he was out or that we had been in contact with him *or* that we had found him so close to our home."

"Damn, Shiloh. You should have told her," Sam said.

"In retrospect, I agree. She was pretty steamed up at me."

"All right, I'll have Madeline cancel or put off any appointments I might have and you have Holly do the same.

"Let's all try to be here at eleven this morning—and you're now part of this investigation, Abernathy—assuming you want in."

"Wouldn't miss it for the world," Tom Abernathy said.

We were gathered around the table in the conference room, where Holly had put out coffee cups, carafes of coffee, and small dishes for the pastries she had ordered for the meeting.

Tom was opposite of myself, flanked by Sam and Jennifer, along with a scroungy-looking little man Sam had introduced as Shorty Pitt, and Al Reagan.

A young technician in gold rimmed glasses had set up a large screen television and readied it to play, but he had not been invited to stay by the Sheriff.

My beautiful housemate, dressed in a sophisticated gray suit and maroon blouse, with her hair loose and large silver hoop earrings showing, had barely nodded in my direction when she came in.

"Does everyone who wants coffee and a pastry have them?" Sam said. "This video runs sixteen minutes and I want everyone to see it all at one sitting."

When everyone at the table nodded affirmatively, Sam switched the video on. Even those of us who had seen the original watched intently because the quality was so much better on the big screen than it had been on small screens.

The sermon started and nobody reacted until the preacher used the words *queer* and *faggot*, which caused a sharp intake of breath from Jennifer.

Al Reagan had sat up and leaned forward as soon as the sermon started. He watched quietly until the same words that Sam and I had recognized, *God, family, and love of country are what the United States was built on...* then he began to curse under his breath and his face grew red and mottled.

Finally, when the recording ran out, Jennifer said, "That is the most vile and disgusting rant I have ever heard!"

"I agree," Sam said. "Now who wants to tell our esteemed lawyer who the preacher is?"

"It's someone you *know*?" Jennifer asked.

Al Reagan cleared his throat and I saw he was polishing his glasses. "That so-called preacher is Patrol Sergeant Larry Wilkin of the Knox County Sheriff's Office, who not so long ago sat in this very room, being interviewed for the lieutenant slot that John Freed got."

"Do you think *he* fired the shot at John's wedding?" Jennifer asked.

"No," Al said, "he was on a traffic stop at Dixie Lee Junction, almost in Loudon County, when that shot was fired, but we may still be able to link him to the shooting. If we can find out if it was carried out by one of his disciples from the Sanctified Gospel Temple, we may be able to nail him as an accessory to murder."

Jennifer turned to Sam and asked, "Why am I here instead of your staff lawyer?"

"Because I don't want the word to leak out that I have any knowledge of Wilkin's activities until I'm ready.

"So my question is this: When I'm ready, can I fire him for conduct unbecoming an officer, Counselor?"

"Yes, you can fire him and be tied up in court for years because this is a First Amendment issue, based on freedom of religion and probably free speech, since it was a private gathering—unless there's something in your Code of Conduct about the use of disparaging language towards fellow officers or the public."

"Shiloh and I both worked on the latest revision of the Code of Conduct. I can fire Wilkin for cowardice, even offensive tattoos and insubordination, but we left out *disparaging language*, because we didn't envision this sort of thing."

"Tom, would you introduce your colleague to the rest of us?" Sam said to the Knoxville Police Department Investigator who had originally brought them the recording.

"Yes, this is my colleague, Criminal Investigator Donovan Pitt, generally known as 'Shorty,'" the tall Denzel Washington look-alike began.

"He is currently working undercover as a homeless man. He got into the Sanctified Gospel Temple by hooking up with a real homeless man who goes there for coffee and cakes and sometimes does odd jobs for the pastor. He's very good at what he does.

"Stand up and talk, Shorty," Abernathy said.

Pitt, a shorter than average man with stringy hair and a ragged beard, wearing ill-fitting clothing and looking nothing like a police officer, stood.

"It took me a while to work my way in because these people are not very welcoming for a so-called church.

"The first two or three times I went in with a real homeless guy, they patted me down for weapons and any kind of recording device, then seemed to accept me for what they thought I was. It was the seventh trip in when I wore a camera and got this video.

"As you can see, there are posters with Old Testament Bible verses about gay people and they have a pamphlet they hand out to scare the hell out of any would-be sinner. What you see in the video is pretty much what every service is like.

"I'll answer questions, if you have any. I don't like this so-called Reverend Wilkin," the undercover officer said. "I'm at your service."

"Sam, Pitt is as good as you were in your undercover days when we called you a chameleon," I said.

"Not as nasty-looking as I used to be, but I wouldn't have made you as a cop, either. I do have a question," Sam said,

"Go ahead, Sheriff," Pitt said.

"I've been over this enhanced video several times already and you got a facial during your sweep of almost everyone, except the guy sitting to the left front, the one in the brown jacket and gray fedora. What can you tell me about him?"

"He never speaks out in meetings, not even to say *Amen*, and he always sits there to the front and apart.

"He appears to be in his early fifties or late forties, around six feet, and appears fit. Wilkin treats him very respectfully.

"I suspect this guy is funding the church because the collection plate never has more than a few dollars in it, and I've seen that guy hand Wilkin fat envelopes on two occasions.

"I can't give you an eye color or even hair color, because that gray fedora is always pulled down low. He gets there early, so he may have a key, though I can't say for sure, and leaves after we do.

"If he has a car, he apparently parks somewhere away from the church lot, and so far I haven't been able to tail him on foot without being obvious."

"Sounds like you've been very thorough, Officer Pitt. Does Wilkin have any leaders within the group?" Al Reagan asked.

"He has two guys he calls deacons, but mostly they just give him a lot of *amens* and take up the collection.

"One of them lives near a gay bar that has been vandalized. I heard him giving directions to his house to another member, but we haven't made a connection yet," Pitt replied.

"Well, that's what we have, folks, unless Officer Pitt can identify the mystery man in the fedora."

"Excuse me, Sheriff," Tom Abernathy said.

"Go ahead, Tom."

"We've held this tape back as long as we can. The report is due in and I can't hold it back any longer without burning Officer Pitt.

"If our esteemed chief of police stays true to character, the news media will have this tape by tomorrow,"

"So, if the tape goes to the media, it's unlikely you'll be able to get Pitt or anyone else back inside that so-called church?"

"That's what I mean, Sheriff," Tom said.

"I guess I'd better get ahead of the Reverend Sergeant Wilkin's coming scandal. Someone get the homophobic bastard in here.

"Chief of Detective Reagan, get his early retirement papers ready, just because he may decide to be rational about this."

"Right away, Sheriff." Reagan put the paper he had been using to polish his glasses in his pocket and left the conference room.

FOURTEEN

Sam and I sat in his office, drinking coffee, looking down at the Tennessee River. The water flowing under the Henley Street and Gay Street Bridge, both visible from the window, had been called the Tennessee River before Knoxville was even a town.

Even though the Tennessee Valley Authority had changed the designation to Fort Loudon Lake, nobody but newspaper editors intent on accuracy paid any attention to the name change.

"The Sergeant should be here any time," Sam said. "I hope he gets rattled enough to tell us who it is that's financing his unholy operation. I think Pitt's probably right that the ragtag group following Wilkin is not raising enough money to even pay the rent."

"I wonder what's keeping Al Reagan," I said.

"He probably stopped to polish his glasses," Sam said. "Everybody has tics, but what's with the polishing papers?"

"Al used to be a heavy smoker. When he occasionally falls off the wagon, the polishing slows down a lot."

"Speak of the devil," Sam said as there was a knock on the office door. "Come on in, Chief of Detectives Reagan."

Al opened the door and looked around. "Am I late?"

"No. Wilkin was working an extra job directing traffic and the Patrol Captain sent someone to pick him up. He should be here any minute now," Sam said.

"Then we'd better get ready," Al said. He picked up a straight-back chair that was against the wall and set it down facing Sam's desk, then got another one and set it at the opposite side of the desk where I was sitting.

"Let's put the bastard on edge by seating him alone and facing the highest-ranking men in this department."

"Good thinking, Al," I said.

At the same moment, there was another knock on the door.

"Come in," Sam said.

The door opened slowly and Sergeant Wilkin, already looking nervous, accompanied by the patrol officer who had brought him in from his job site, hesitantly entered.

"Sergeant, take a seat *there*. Officer, thanks for bringing him in. If you will stand guard outside the door and make sure nobody disturbs us."

The patrol officer, looking relieved, stepped out in the hall and closed the door.

Sergeant Wilkin took a seat, looked at the three of us, and swallowed hard.

"Chief Tempest, will you turn on that widescreen television on the table to your left?" Sam said. "Sergeant, can you see the screen?"

"Yes, Sheriff, I can see it."

"Then sit quietly and watch it without speaking until you're asked a question." Sam nodded at me and I pushed the start button.

Wilkin swallowed hard again and went even paler than he already was as soon as the video started. We sat quietly and let the entire sixteen minutes play out.

When it ended, Wilkin started to speak. "Sheriff—"

"Did anyone ask you a question, Sergeant?"

"No, Sheriff."

"Then shut the hell up!" Sam said.

Sam stretched the silence out another two minutes, watching Wilkin squirm.

"Well, *Parson* Wilkin, that was some sermon. Do you believe the crap you were saying or is someone paying you to say it?" Sam asked.

"Sheriff..." Wilkin was stammering. "I have freedom of religion..."

"Don't you dare throw the First Amendment at me," Sam said. "This department has a Code of Conduct and a regulation against demeaning or slandering another employee of this department—and I haven't *decided* what I'm going to do with you.

"Did you know about the regulation that prohibits demeaning or slandering?" Sam asked.

"Yes, Sheriff, I knew, but I didn't mention any individual by name..."

"You really didn't have to *name* anyone. *Queers*, *faggots*, and *perverts* are terms often used to express hatred for homosexual people, and that includes at least one of your fellow officers, a brave and dedicated cop," I said.

"As I recall, you asked him in my presence when he was getting married."

Wilkin's eyes suddenly narrowed. "I had nothing to do with what happened at Freed's wedding. Do I need a lawyer?"

"Nobody has mentioned John's wedding but you, *Parson* Wilkin," Sam said. "And did anyone Mirandize you?"

"No, sir, but I can tell you exactly where I was when that shooting went down."

"We already know *exactly* where you were—on a traffic stop, Wilkin. That's why you haven't been Mirandized," I said. "If you cooperate with us, we can help ease you out gracefully," Sam said.

"How do you mean *cooperate?*"

"We think you're a *patsy*, not smart enough to attract a congregation. We want the name of the guy in the fedora, the one who always sits in the same seat up front and never says anything, not even *amen*. We think he's the brains and the money behind the Sanctified Gospel Temple. Give us his name and we'll make things a lot easier for you."

Wilkin dropped his eyes downward before speaking. "I can't do that."

"Come on, son," Al Reagan said. "Counting your military service, you've got over twenty years and until now a clean record. Don't go out in disgrace!"

"I can't risk my mortal soul," Wilkin said. "This department is aiding and abetting gross immorality that's contrary to the will of God and I don't want to be judged along with you."

"I'm pretty sure this guy isn't the *Pope*," Sam said.

"Mock me all you want," Wilkin said. "God will judge me, not you."

"I certainly hope God judges you. But today I am rendering my judgment," Sam said. "Here's the deal. You request early retirement *right now* and you can leave with your pension intact and your reputation in tatters. If you *don't* sign your early retirement papers before you leave today, I'll fire you for conduct unbecoming an officer and violation the Code of Conduct. We'll probably spend *years* in court while you defend your First Amendment rights, and during that time, everyone else in this room will be drawing a salary and have health insurance, but you won't. I will also ask the Peace Officers Standards and Training Commission to revoke your law enforcement credentials and you'll never work as a cop again. You do remember the P.O.S.T. Commission, don't you?"

"I understand what you're saying," Wilkin said. "I'll sign the early retirement papers." He was staring at the floor.

"Good," Sam said. "Put your badge, credentials, and weapon on my desk. Chief Reagan has the paperwork.

"Go to the conference room, sign the papers, and Chief Reagan will go with you to personnel to make sure you actually keep your word. Right now, your credentials, badge, and weapon on my desk—*then get out of my sight.*"

Only another cop would have noticed that Sam, Reagan, and I had shifted almost imperceptibly in our seats so that we could more easily reach our weapons in case Wilkin blew up. The now former sergeant had once been a real cop, so he noticed.

A minute later, Wilkin's credentials, badge, and weapon were on Sam's desk, and the door closed as Wilkin and Reagan left.

"Is everything in place?" Sam asked.

"A tracking device has been installed in Wilkin's civilian car that he drove to his side job today because he turned his cruiser in to be serviced yesterday. Al will clone his phone with a little device your electronics genius left with us, while he and Wilkin are standing side by side in the personnel office, and it's legal because the phone belongs to the department.

"And three undercover units will be on the former sergeant's tail when he leaves the job site where he left his car. If he calls our mystery man or goes to him in the next couple of days, we'll know who he is."

"When have you heard from our newlyweds?" Sam asked.

"Well, John has called several times for updates. The last call was an hour ago to tell me he will be back to work in the morning."

"Have you kept him updated?"

"No. I didn't want him to get excited and come home to get in our way. You know how excitable John is."

"I'm learning," Sam said. "Let's burn one to celebrate," he said, getting the old metal ashtray out of his desk drawer.

Jennifer's red BMW sportster was already in the driveway when I arrived home.

She had balked on driving it when I bought it without telling her, but she eventually let me talk her into it. She had flatly refused to allow me to buy a personalized TEMPEST 2 tag to go along with *my* personal tag, TEMPEST 1. She said it would be like wearing a sign that said SHILOH'S GIRL.

Magdala's head popped up in the kitchen window, so I knew she would be waiting at the door, sniffing until she sneezed, by the time I got there.

As I inserted my key, I heard Magdala whining and sniffing, but as the door opened, I also caught a delicious odor emanating from the kitchen.

"It's good to see you, too, Magdala." I grabbed her by the ears and rubbed them briskly as she sighed in near ecstasy. "But I have to wonder if you're excited to see me or is your mouth watering from the food I smell."

"Probably both," Jennifer said entering the kitchen clad in white shorts and a yellow halter top. "Make room for the *compañera*, Magdala."

Without warning Jennifer slithered into my arms with the slinkiness of a cat, and kissed me deeply.

As she stepped back, I said, "Whoa, that took my breath away. What have I done to earn it?"

"Just by being you, *señor policía*. I've behaved badly and wanted to make it up to you."

"You *cooked* for me?"

"Don't be silly. You know I don't cook. I called El Chico as soon as I knew you were leaving the office, and it's still very hot. I know it's Tex-Mex and not Mexican, but I talked to them in advance and they said they'd have it ready: tortilla soup, chile rellenos, tamales, and chicken fajitas with rice and beans on the side. *All* your favorites."

"But how did you know when I'd be leaving?"

"Holly tipped me off."

"The women in my life take care of me. And you, too, Magdala. *Calm down* and stop dancing."

I put some of the chicken in Magdala's dish as Jennifer opened two ice-cold Negra Modelo beers, our favorite Mexican beer that was first brewed by

Austrian immigrants to Mexico who had previously brewed lager back at home.

"Don't wolf your food," I said to Magdala, knowing she wouldn't listen.

Jennifer and I ate quietly, enjoying our food and dark Mexican beer. She had ordered extra chile rellenos for me, knowing how much I like them, even though they were neither from Texas or Mexico, but from New Mexico.

Magdala had wolfed her chicken down and sat expectantly staring at the two of us. She is an optimist.

"Shiloh, do you want to get married?"

"Not unless you do, *mi amor*. I know how you treasure your privacy and independence," I answered, taking a bite of tamale.

"Shiloh, my love, you have always been fierce, but steady. You don't act impulsively. And when your normal behavior changes it worries us. Not necessarily *big* things, but things that stand out…"

"Did Sam tell you, or did JoAnn from personnel call and tell you I had changed my insurance and retirement into your name?" I took another bite of tamale and washed it down with the cold beer.

"Shiloh, he's worried—and so am I."

"I am now resigned to never keeping anything, no matter how personal, a secret."

"Don't be *angry*. I started worrying when you first brought up marriage again. But I've thought it over and I think I'm being unreasonable."

"Do I look angry?"

"No, and you can't keep a secret from the people who love you most," she answered.

"Not when one of my friends is the Sheriff of Knox County, and everyone else close to me is worried."

"Sam probably told you I offered to take a psych evaluation. As for marriage, when I'm convinced it's what *you* want and not because you're worried about my mental health, *then* we can talk about it again. This was a great meal."

"Shiloh, if we *do* get married, it will be with the understanding that I remain Jennifer Mendoza. My professional career has been made under my maiden name."

"Of course, no label that says *Shiloh's girl*."
"Are you up for dessert, my little rooster?" she asked.
"As long as it isn't too heavy."
"I weigh one hundred and twelve pounds," she said.
"Then by all means, dish it up."

FIFTEEN

"Al, are you trying to tell me that you caught Todd Aiken within shooting distance of my wedding, and he has convinced you he was there as one of the good guys?"

Lieutenant John Freed was back from his brief honeymoon, fired up and ready for action. I paused outside the Chief of Detective's office to listen before going in.

"Yes, John, and he gave us a good lead on the shooter. It's all in the file here. Catch up and take over your case," Al said, winking in my direction as I stood just outside his partially-open door.

"And *nobody* filled me in. I've been calling Shiloh regularly." John sounded like a child who had not been invited to a birthday party.

"Shiloh didn't want to ruin your honeymoon—or rather CJ's honeymoon—because he already knew where your mind was."

"I just can't believe it, after all we've been through together since the Chief came out of retirement," John said.

"Believe it, *Lieutenant*. It was for the good of your new marriage. You need to understand that the job is not your reason for living. It just pays the bills. Did CJ enjoy the trip?"

"I have to admit that he did, Chief," John said, turning to look at me. "It was a swanky place the Sheriff paid for. We definitely couldn't have afforded it otherwise."

"Well, mission accomplished, Lieutenant. Take the case file and catch up. Spend some time on that video, and maybe you'll see something we missed."

"Copy that, Boss." John stood and reached into his pocket and handed me a plastic key chain. "I saw this and thought of you Chief."

I turned over the plastic part of the key chain and read the words:

"Yea though I walk through the Valley of the Shadow of Death, I will fear no evil Because I am the meanest sonofabitch in the valley..."

"Thank you, John. Now get moving."

"Right away, Chief." The tall redheaded lieutenant went back to the corner where Reagan had already prepared a board for posting accumulated evidence.

At the top was a picture of Sergeant Wilkin, who, though not a direct suspect, was the opening act.

"What did John bring you from Gatlinburg, Al?" I asked.

Al took another key chain similar to mine from his desk drawer. His had a picture of a gorilla with a baseball bat that said: *"Play ball with me or I'll shove this bat up your ass."*

"John has a cop's ironic sense of humor, Al." Anybody who knows, understands that this is just cop bravado, not how he really feels. What do think he brought for the Sheriff?"

"I don't know, but whatever it is, Sam will pretend to like it."

"All right, I just wanted to welcome our newlywed back. I knew he'd be early today. I'm on my way up to see Sam and check on what the grapevine has put out about Wilkin's resignation. I mean *early retirement*."

"The grapevine is fully functional from the secretarial pool all the way to jail staff. Everyone knows he left against his will because he's somehow connected to the shooting at John and CJ's wedding."

"And those who *don't* know can walk through here and see Wilkin's picture on the perp board," I said.

"I didn't think it would compromise the case and I got a great deal of satisfaction from posting his picture. And who knows, somebody within the department may have pertinent information," Al said, taking out his little pack of tissue papers to polish his glasses.

"Al, you have a streak of vindictiveness I had never suspected."

"It comes out when someone tries to hurt my friends, Shiloh. I take it very personally."

"I see that now, Al. Well, I'll go up and talk to Sam."

As I was about to knock on the private door to Sam's office, it opened and I met Lieutenant Cliff Sajak, the Echo Shift Commander, coming out.

He is a man of medium height, fortyish with graying hair, known for being a strict disciplinarian—and until yesterday, had been the former Sergeant Wilkin's direct supervisor.

"Excuse me, Chief," he said.

I nodded and said, "Good morning, Lieutenant."

When I entered, the Sheriff, dressed in a black suit, black loafers, a pearl gray shirt, and pale yellow silk tie, was placing a fresh cup of coffee on the front of his desk. The old battered metal ashtray was already in sight.

"I was just putting your coffee out, Chief Tempest, black with two artificial sweeteners."

"Have you become clairvoyant, Sheriff?"

"No, Al called to see what Freed brought me back from Gatlinburg and said you were on your way up. That's John's gift on the side of my desk."

John's gift to the Sheriff was similar to the key chains he had bought for me and Al, except it was a framed picture under glass with a drawing of a butterfly and the following words:

"If you love something, set it free. If it comes back, it's yours. If it doesn't, you can always hunt it down and kill it."

"Does John Freed not understand that we all are onto him as a softhearted man who would not swat a flea unless he couldn't avoid it?" Sam asked me.

"Well, he's been a cop since he turned legal age, and he's always been known for being jumpy and excitable, Sam. So he tries to blend in. Not to play shrink, but being gay has more than likely made him feel like a total outsider, so he wants to give the appearance of being a badass."

"We gonna light up? By the way he also bought me some nice silver cufflinks with an "R" monogram on them."

"Wow, that surprises me."

"It surprised me, too," Sam said. "He purchased them in the hotel gift shop and charged them to his room account."

I was about to take a sip of coffee, but was glad I hadn't because Sam would have had coffee spewed all over his desk.

"Nobody said he was *sophisticated* in the ways of the world, Sam. He meant well." I slid my cigarettes and lighter across the desk.

"I see Wilkin's supervisor was in here to assure you he knew nothing about the sergeant's homophobic little temple."

Sam lit his cigarette, then slid the pack and my lighter back to me.

"Not just Wilkin's supervisor, but also the commanders of David and Adam shifts have been by to tell me they knew nothing about Wilkin's extracurricular activities. *Nobody* wants the stink of this thing on them," Sam said.

"The word hit the grapevine quicker than usual. I wonder who was first to put the word out?"

"Well, you and I both have secretaries—not *implying*, just mentioning. Several people saw the Sergeant walk out with Al, minus his badge and weapon. And Personnel Division has several people who saw it. And who knows? Maybe Wilkin told his friends, if he has any." Sam said.

"Now all anyone has to do is walk into the Detective Division and see the Sergeant's picture on top of the lead board by John's desk."

Sam appeared startled for a moment, then took another drag off his cigarette and smiled.

"Al continues to surprise with every case we work," Sam said. "And it's not like there are ever any *real* secrets."

There was a knock on the door and Sam put out his cigarette, passed the ashtray to me to put mine out, and then irritably put the ashtray back in his desk drawer.

"Come in," Sam said.

The door opened, and Chief of Personnel Lance Wittaker entered.

"How can I help you today, Chief?" Sam asked.

"Since everyone seems to know what Sergeant Larry Wilkin was doing, I wanted to tell you that I had no idea he was running his little outlaw church when I recommended him for the lieutenant's slot. I guess I'm not as good a judge of character as I once thought."

"He had us all fooled, Lance. It hadn't crossed our minds that you had any knowledge of what he was doing off-duty—not any more than anyone else who interviewed him."

"Thank you, Sheriff. I just wanted to make sure that you didn't think Wilkin and I were anything but casual acquaintances."

"Rest assured, Chief. None of us thought your recommendation was based on anything but what appeared to be the former sergeant's sterling record," Sam said.

"Thank you, Sheriff." He nodded in my direction. "I'll let you two get back to business."

"It must be true that cops always feel guilty," Sam said. "Should I post a notice of absolution on my door and stop all the denials from people who had nothing to do with Wilkin's little homophobic church?"

Before I could answer, Sam's cell phone began to play the theme song from the film *Bad Boys*. He answered and listened intently.

"Thanks," he said, then looking at me continued: "In the words of Alice, 'This gets curiouser and curiouser.'"

"Who was that?" I asked.

"A trustworthy source in records."

"You have an *informant* in the records bureau in a department of which you are the boss?"

"Of course, I do. The personnel in records division have bosses. I just make sure I have a loyal set of ears that contacts me *earlier*, or maybe more than one. I'm quite charming, you know."

"Okay, Mister Slick, what did your source in records just tell you?"

"Former Sergeant Larry Wilkin's wife called and said he went out target shooting yesterday evening and didn't come home. Apparently he didn't tell the wife about his early retirement, either."

"Let Al and me handle this before the new Lieutenant finds out about it. John's still a little shaky when it comes to dealing with Wilkin."

"Have at it. I'll make sure it doesn't go to John's desk before you talk to Wilkin's wife," Sam said.

"Where did you tell John you were going?" I said as we left the City-County Building in my old maroon Ford cruiser.

"I told him I have a doctor's appointment and that he's in charge until I get back," Al said.

"I don't have a good feeling about this, Al. Wilkin is not the most stable person I've ever met, and he's the only link we have with whoever was funding his little church of horrors."

"I know. When he didn't give up his sponsor, I knew we were dealing with a true believer, willing to trash his career rather than give up the money man."

"Fanatics are always a wild card, Al, because they're unpredictable.

"Did you want to stop for a sandwich on the way to Wilkin's place? It's almost to the Jefferson County line."

"Not unless you do, Shy. I had a sandwich I brought from home about nine this morning. If I bring my own lunch I don't end up over-eating at Szechuan Garden on Chapman Highway."

"They do have good food, Al. Do you remember when Bamboo Chinese Palace was the only Asian place in South Knoxville? It was right down from where Szechuan Garden is now."

"Yeah, they had one hell of a buffet at Bamboo Chinese Palace. You took me and John there once when you first came back to the department. Don't you remember how hard it was to get John to just *try* Asian cuisine?"

"I had forgotten that, but man did he put it away after he had a taste of sweet and sour chicken. Yeah, I really liked Bamboo Chinese Palace.

"I wonder what happened to such a successful place, Al."

"I heard the owner was abusive and his wife divorced him and married his best cook. She had a successful place out north for a while. Her new husband made the best hot and sour sauce in this county."

"Taste of Malaysia. Yeah, I remember that place but I never made the connection. They *did* have the best hot and sour soup in Knoxville. Now it makes sense.

"Al, have you ever noticed that the older we get, the better the good old days look?"

"Yeah, I guess the younger we were the better things tasted and smelled."

"You know, Al, that's been on my mind a lot lately…"

"Take the next exit," Al said, then to the left."

"I haven't been here in a long time," I said. "There's a fairly famous general store down the road."

"Yeah, not surprisingly, it's called *The General Store*, Shiloh."

"I walked right into that one didn't I, Al?"

"What were you saying when I interrupted you, Boss?"

"Hell, Al, I don't know. Must not have been important. The road where Wilkin lives is just down the road to the right, if I remember correctly."

Ten minutes later, we pulled into the long driveway leading to a remodeled farm house, painted white with red trim, which had been common in East Tennessee just after World War ll.

"Looks like the Wilkins keep their place well cared for," Al said.

"Also looks as if Wilkin's wife is expecting us," I said.

A thin woman with her hair back in a bun, looking older than I expected, had come out on the front porch. She was wearing an apron with flowers on it over a checked dress.

"Did you tell her we were coming, Shy?"

"No, but I'd say she expected to see someone after she reported that her husband hadn't come home last night," I said.

We walked the short distance to the porch and paused at the steps. "Mrs. Wilkin, I'm Chief Deputy Shiloh Tempest and this is Al Reagan, Chief of Detectives."

"I've heard Larry speak of both of you," she said. "Come on in and I'll fetch ya'll a cup of coffee."

"Mrs. Wilkin, your husband has a very elaborate pistol range behind the house," I said.

"Yes, he spends a lot of money on it, and a lot of time practicing. Ya'll can call me Ethyl. Come in please."

Up close, my estimate of her age changed. I had thought she was perhaps in her mid-forties. But a closer look caused me to change my estimate to middle or late thirties—but a woman who did not spend a lot of time or money pampering herself.

"Have a seat," she said, "and I'll bring in the coffee."

Both Al and I were familiar enough with rural people to know we would have coffee placed in front of us because it was part of rural culture to be sociable.

As we waited, I looked around and saw that the furniture was also traditional, nothing of the modernistic, or what a person with a rural upbringing would consider "fancy."

The television was a flat screen, but sat on a sturdy, wooden coffee table, not a viewing center with room for disks.

Ethyl, a name that had not been popular since the Great Depression, came in with a standing serving tray holding a carafe, two cups and sugar and cream. She carefully put it in front of us.

"Help yourself. I've had my fill of coffee this morning," she said, pushing her hair back self-consciously.

"Thank you, Ethyl," I said. "You told our dispatcher that Larry went out to shoot last evening and didn't come home. Does that happen often?"

"No. He's always been good about keeping me informed about his whereabouts, even after he started spending time at that so-called church of his."

Her contempt was so clear that Al and I both glanced at each other with slightly narrowed eyes.

"I take it you aren't a member of that church," I said.

"No, I'm not. I'm a Pentecostal, Assemblies of God. So was Larry until he started doing Bible study with a friend he always call the rabbi, who I never met. It was after that he said he got the call to preach."

"Rabbi?" Al said.

We both knew a rabbi is a Jewish clergyman, a teacher, and Larry was definitely using the New Testament, at least fragments of it in his so-called ministry.

"That's the only name Larry ever used," she said.

"Mrs. Wilkin... I mean Ethyl... How was Larry's new church different from The Assemblies of God?" Al asked, taking a sip of coffee.

"We're strict about holiness. But we're about *love* not *hate*. I read the trash pamphlets he was bringing home and his so-called sermon notes—and they disgusted me!"

"You wouldn't have any of those sermon notes would you, Ethyl?"

"No, Chief Tempest. I made him take that trash out of my home. After that, he kept that stuff in a box in the trunk of his cruiser. He had left it at the service center for an oil change, so I don't know where it is now."

"Ethyl, did Larry tell you he retired yesterday?" I asked.

"God, no! I thought he just left his cruiser to be serviced. He *retired?*"

"Yes," I replied.

"We had calculated he had to work five more years before we could *afford* for him to retire. Did it have something to do with that unholy church he was involved with?"

"It's not something I can discuss with you. I'm sorry. Why did Larry go somewhere to shoot when he has a nice range out back?" I asked.

"He only used that range for pistol shooting. He took his rifle with him yesterday evening."

"Excuse me," Al said. "Someone is trying to call me and I'm getting interference on my cell phone. I'll try getting through outside on the porch."

"Of course, Chief Reagan, go ahead." I watched the big man shuffle out, knowing a call hadn't come in on his cell phone. We all have individual ring tones. Mine is *The Sting*. Al's is the song *I Fought the Law, and the Law Won*.

"Do you and Larry have children, Ethyl?" I asked, hoping to distract her before she also realized that Al's phone had not rung.

"We had a still-born little girl ten years ago. I was never able to be with child after that." Tears sprang to her eyes.

"I'm sorry to hear that, Ethyl. Do you know where Larry and his friend did their rifle shooting?"

She took a tissue from her apron pocket and dried the tears from her eyes.

"No, Chief Tempest, but it's only about a fifteen-minute drive, wherever it is. I've timed him a lot after he called to tell me he was on his way home."

The door opened and Al stuck his head in the door. "Chief Tempest, we're needed back at headquarters."

"Ethyl, if you'll excuse us. We'll have patrol start looking for Larry as soon as we leave. You've been very helpful."

She stood on the porch and watched as Al and I drove away. As always, I felt a pang of guilt at deceiving a worried family member. Sometimes it's unavoidable, though.

"Wilkin's cruiser is being towed from the service center where he left it to be serviced, to the lab people downtown."

"Good work, now call the lab back and have them look in the trunk for his sermon notes and pull the GPS tracking system on that cruiser. We're looking for a location frequently visited that's within fifteen minutes of his house. And while you're doing that, I'm going to drive us back down to The General Store to get us a snack. I'm thinking of one of those 'best barbecue sandwiches in America' they're advertising."

"Got it," Al said as I was finishing what might arguably have been *one* of the best barbecue sandwiches in America, and my Dr. Pepper that had come from a round galvanized wash tub filled with ice.

"No sermon notes in his cruiser, but there's a subdivision that was laid out years ago, then abandoned, three miles from the Wilkin house. No road names yet, but there's a long cul-de-sac that looks like it might be perfect for target practice.

SIXTEEN

"**You always hear** about how much money there is to be made in real estate, then you find what was supposed to be a classy subdivision, probably a gated community, that someone has abandoned after spending only God knows how much money," Al said as we slowly explored the abandoned property.

"I'm just a cop who writes books on the side, Al. Economics is not my strong suit."

"Are you *really* a cop who writes on the side or a writer who found a job where he never has to work another day because he loves it?"

"You're digging deep, Al. That's not like you when you aren't working a case."

"The cul-de-sac should be around this curve on the right, Shy. I always meant to ask you that question. It's like somebody offered me a job to do nothing but hunting and fishing. In that case, I would never work another day and still get paid."

"Al, I can't answer that question. I thought I was doing all right before Sam enticed me back to the job. I don't need the money, but I'm still here."

"There's a car parked about two hundred yards down the cul-de-sac. Wilkin's car is an older model Chevrolet, muscle car," Al said.

"That looks like a metallic blue 1970 Chevelle," I said.

"That's definitely a muscle car and there's somebody on the driver's side," I said, stopping about fifty yards away to avoid contaminating the scene.

"Grab a couple pairs of rubber gloves out of my glove box, Al. Whoever is in the car hasn't moved."

We drew our weapons. just in case somebody was playing possum to sucker us in, and slowly approached the Chevelle—I from the driver's side and Al from the passenger's side.

When I was about fifteen feet away, I saw the spatter of blood, brains, and bone fragments on the driver's side car window, as I had seen many times before, and relaxed.

"He's dead, Al." I holstered my weapon. "Looks like a head wound delivered from the passenger side."

Al eased up to the passenger side and looked in, then holstered his weapon.

"Wound to the temple. Looks like a Glock pistol has fallen out of his hand and is partially wedged beside the bucket seat," Al said. "The round is somewhere in the car, because it hit the upper door frame and ricocheted. It's Larry Wilkin," Al said, pulling on rubber gloves.

"Let's take a quick look, being very careful," I said, putting on the other pair of rubber gloves. "I want a pristine crime scene when the crime techs and medical examiner get here."

"I think I can reach the keys without disturbing anything," Al said, opening the passenger side door. He reached over carefully and pulled the keys from the ignition with his gloved fingers.

We walked around to the rear of the gleaming Chevelle, which Wilkin had obviously spent a lot of time restoring to pristine condition, and opened the trunk.

There was what appeared to be an AR-15, a semiautomatic version of the military M-16, but with a scope attached. We left it in the trunk for the crime scene techs to process.

"I don't see anything that looks like sermon notes. He must have another place where he stashed things," I said.

"Or somebody carried them off, Al."

"Shiloh, this looks like a straight-up suicide"

"It does, and it may be, but let me run a thought past you. Most of us in this business consider ourselves a part of a glorified warrior culture..."

"Who fall on our swords rather than face shame and disgrace. I *know*, and it looks like this is what Wilkin did," Al responded.

"We've both seen officers take this way out, Al. What's the term?"

"We orally copulate with our weapons, eat them to insure there's hopefully no pain."

"And why do we do it that way?"

"Because we learn from our rookie training that the only way to cause *instant* death in a suspect is to separate the brain from the body.

"How many hours do we train that as a last resort to take a *handkerchief shot*, that invisible twelve-inch square over a hostage's right shoulder when a perp has a pistol to his or her head, Al?"

"For the same reason we eat our pistols, Shiloh—because even with a fatal head wound, if the brain stem, that point right under the nose and below the brain, isn't destroyed instantly, a lot of movement and maybe agonizing pain is possible."

"We may never prove that Larry Wilkin didn't fall on his own sword, but I'm thinking this secret *rabbi* who taught Larry his twisted view of scripture is still around, tying up loose ends."

"We've always called a senior officer who takes interest in a young cop and tries to smooth the way for him—like you did for both me and John Freed—a rabbi, but with no religious overtones, Shiloh."

"And it may be that Wilkin actually used it in a religious sense also, Al. But I'm going to need some strong reassurances that the guy bankrolling that so-called church isn't still lurking in the background, tying up loose ends."

"The techs and medical examiner will be here soon, Boss. If you would like to head in and update the Sheriff, I'll guard the crime scene."

"That makes sense, Al, but..."

"Make sure the technicians scour the area for shell casings and any other evidence, as well as fingerprints and spatter. I remember how to work a crime scene, Shiloh."

"I know you do, Al. Didn't mean to imply otherwise. You know if I could sink a steering wheel into the Earth and steer the entire planet I would."

"That's what makes you so endearing, Boss. You head back in and I'll see that everything gets done. By the way, you know Lieutenant Freed will be very upset that we jumped his call," Al said.

"I'm well aware, Chief Reagan."

I found the Sheriff, leaning back in his chair, staring out at the Tennessee River.

"Come in, Shiloh. John Freed has already been in, bitching about you and Al jumping a crucial call in his case."

"And you told him?"

"I told him it was your decision. And when the case is solved he can make the arrest—if possible. It was as close to insubordinate as I've ever seen him."

"I know, but I was afraid he still was too much on edge to interview Wilkin's wife."

"Good call, Shiloh. Did Wilkin actually eat his gun?"

"No, the round went into his right temple and slightly upward. He probably didn't die instantly, Sam."

"Very sloppy suicide for a professional gunfighter," Sam said.

"That's my thought, but if he had possibly been firing the handgun prior to that—which his wife indicated was what he went out to do—if so, he's going to have powder residue on his right hand and we may never be able to prove he didn't fire the fatal shot.

"And one more thing—Wilkin's wife said that the problems began when he started doing Bible study with a friend he called his *rabbi*."

"Interesting choice of words," Sam said. "A Jewish religious teacher and a cop mentor."

"My thought, exactly, Sam."

"Maybe the crime scene techs will find something that will throw light on the entire subject," Sam said.

"Maybe. May I borrow your ashtray, Boss." I said.

"I will if you'll give me a cigarette and a light."

Sam took his old battered ashtray out of its drawer and we both lit up, then sat quietly for a few minutes.

"How many cop suicides have you worked, Shiloh?"

"Too many."

"Yeah, one would have been too many."

As Sam was putting away the ashtray, his secretary, Madeline, buzzed the intercom. "Sheriff, Lieutenant Freed's husband is asking to see you."

Sam looked at me, raised his right eyebrow, and said, "Send him in."

The door opened and CJ entered. Seeing both of us, he looked startled for a second. We had only seen the tall, blond, and thirtyish young man on social occasions, never in the office before.

"Thanks for seeing me without an appointment," he said. "And first, let me thank both of you for what you've done for John—and especially for the trip to Gatlinburg, Sheriff."

"No thanks needed. John is a valued member of this department and a member of our police family. Pull up a chair, CJ," Sam said, "and tell us how we can help you."

CJ picked up a chair from along the wall and put it in front of Sam's desk. We waited for a moment and, seeing that we were waiting, the young man finally spoke.

"John has been very upset and obsessed with the murder of Pastor Wilson because he thinks it has something to do with our wedding."

"Neither of you is responsible for the actions of a deranged man, CJ. But I know John has taken it personally, so I'm watching the situation closely. Not because John isn't competent, but because it *is* personal for him," I said.

"That's why I'm here—and I hope John doesn't have to know I came in behind his back."

"We won't tell him, CJ, but there's a grapevine here you wouldn't believe, so you might want to tell him yourself," Sam said.

"I can say I came by to see him. But what I'm getting at is that John isn't usually *pushy*, but he's not himself and I'm afraid he may inadvertently offend one of his superiors without meaning to. He does *love* this job."

"I've known few people less pushy than John. Rest assured we are taking everything into consideration with the knowledge of the kind of stress he's under," I said.

The young man seemed to relax a little. "I really appreciate this. Because John has all the respect in the world for the two of you and Chief Reagan. I don't know what he would do if he lost his job."

"CJ, we aren't going to let that happen," Sam said. "Why don't you go out to the lobby and take the elevator to Level 3. There's a buzzer on the door marked Detective Division. Tell them who you are and they'll let you in.

"You can explain to John you just came by to visit him. He'll probably catch you up on the latest information," Sam said.

"You, of course, came by my office to ask permission to go down. If someone saw you here, that's your explanation for being in here."

"I don't know how to thank either of you," CJ said, rising from his chair. "When our relationship was exposed, John thought for sure he'd have to resign, but you were there for him, Chief Tempest."

"I wouldn't have had it any other way, CJ. Just take care of him the best you can," I said.

When the young man had left the office, Sam turned to me. "I'm glad we were able to ease his mind. Do you think we can get John through this before he has a nervous breakdown?"

"I'm going to do my best, Sam."

Jennifer and I began to clear the table and Magdala sighed deeply, aware that there would be no more tidbits of chicken from the Bojangles box I had brought home for dinner.

"Magdala, you act as if you're always on the brink of starvation," Jennifer said.

Our German shepherd's eyes turned into limpid pools of despair and she dropped to the floor with her muzzle on her paws and sighed again.

"Drama Queen," Jennifer said. "Shy, do you want to have our coffee and sweet potato pie now, or do you want to take them to the rec room?"

"Let's have them here. They should go well with the new blend of Kenyan coffee I just brewed."

"Gourmet coffee and Bojangles sweet potato pie. Nobody can accuse you of having *exclusive* tastes," Jennifer said, getting two clear glass Irish coffee mugs and placing them on the counter.

I had read somewhere that glass mugs retain heat better than anything else coffee mugs are made of and Jennifer had kept a supply ever since.

"That's true, you can take the boy away from peasant fare, but you can't take the peasant out of the boy. I love sweet potato pie," I said.

Jennifer put the steaming mugs on the table, and sat down. She was wearing light blue shorts and a light blue halter top, hair pulled back in a ponytail and barefooted, as she often is.

"You didn't have much to say during dinner, *Jefe*. You must be deep into your case."

"You're right. I'm deep in the case and in keeping John sane until it's solved. He's decided that Al and I are jumping his leads because we don't trust him." I took a cautious sip of the Kenyan coffee.

"That's partially true, isn't it?"

"Yes, it is. I should have given the case to someone else. John's too personally involved, but I thought we would wrap it up quicker than this."

"A genuine *whodunnit?*" Jennifer said.

"It appears so. I've been chewing over the fact that Wilkin apparently called his co-conspirator *rabbi*. This is a term that could be a religious thing or for a senior officer who helps a younger officer get ahead by pulling strings."

"Or perhaps both." Jennifer said, taking a delicate sip of coffee.

"You're right. The man in the gray fedora could very well be the money behind that evil little church *and* a cop..."

"With sniper training," Jennifer said.

"Damn, Jennifer! If he's a police sniper, it will be in his folder. It was right in front of my eyes and I didn't see it."

"Neither did anyone else, Shy. But don't go off on a tear. It will wait until morning."

"I know." I also knew I wasn't likely to sleep again, until I was able to get to work.

SEVENTEEN

I put the Hardee's steak and biscuit and coffee I had picked up on my way to work on my desk.

After a sleepless night, I had finally gotten up at five o'clock, dressed quietly, let Magdala out to relieve herself, kissed a still sleepy Jennifer goodbye, and probably violated the speed limit on the way to the office.

I turned on my laptop, sipped coffee, and took a bite of steak and biscuit while waiting for the computer to warm up. It was slow because I had not recently cleared the junk out of it.

The inner door to my office opened and Holly, a startled expression on her face, entered. It occurred to me that I had never seen her without perfect makeup and neatly combed hair.

"Why are you here so early, Chief Tempest?" she asked.

"Why are *you* here so early, Holly?"

"I come in at six so I can take a whole hour off for lunch and still leave at four."

"You don't have to do that, Holly. You can take a full hour without coming in early."

"It's sort of become a routine now, Chief."

She went straight to my coffee maker and turned it on, apparently having set it up before she left yesterday, as usual. *I need to check on getting her a raise.*

"Holly, can you get me into the personnel files?"

"Of course, or I can look up what you need and print it out," she said.

"That's all right, I just need to do some research."

She leaned over my desk and hit a few keys, reminding me how sweet young women can smell. I immediately purged the thought from my mind.

"Give me your password, Chief."

"I don't have one. I've never accessed personnel files before."

"I'll use mine and set you up with your own later, Chief."

She tapped in a string of letters. "It's pretty standard once you get in. You type in the data you need and the computer does the rest. *F9* brings you back to the main page."

"Thank you, Holly. Will you let me know when Chief Reagan comes in?"

"He pulled into the garage right behind me, Chief. Shall I tell him to come in?"

"Am I the only one who drags in here at eight o'clock?"

"No, some of us just are morning people."

"Call him, then, and tell him to come up here as soon as he can."

"Let me set out the coffee cups and cream and sugar first," she said.

"Holly, I've been telling you since we started working together that I don't expect you to be a waitress."

"I know that, Chief. That's why I don't mind doing it."

"Send Al up and I'll get the coffee ready. And if I haven't told you lately—and I probably haven't—I appreciate the efficient way you do things."

She dimpled up and left my office, leaving a swirl of honeysuckle scent in the room.

A few minutes later, Al knocked on my outer door and came in without waiting for me to answer.

"What are you doing here so early, Boss?"

"Trying to keep up with my staff, Al."

"There are morning people and not morning people. Holly and I are morning people. What are you into?"

"My Latina roommate pointed out last night that I should check personnel files to see how many snipers we have in this department."

"We both missed that thought. Hopefully it would have occurred to one of us eventually," Al said.

"Sometimes you can be too close to the forest to see the trees, Al. A fresh perspective can make the difference."

"Any luck so far?" Al asked.

"We have two police trained snipers on the SWAT team, but I already knew about them and both were on the clock and accounted for on the day of the wedding."

"You're looking for the man in the gray fedora, aren't you?"

"Why do you ask, Al?"

"The SWAT guys are both in their twenties and I was looking at the video for the fiftieth time when Holly called. Todd Aiken described the shooter as in the forty to fifty range.

"There's something familiar about that guy, but no matter how often I look at the video, I can't put my finger on it.

"We may end up calling in some of the other parishioners. We've already talked to the so called deacons and they both swear they don't know the guy's name and can't or won't even give us a good description.

"By the way, have you seen the morning paper?" Al asked.

"No. Bad news?"

"That law enforcement genius, Chief Hodge, from the Knoxville P D did exactly what Abernathy said he would do, only faster than we expected. It's on the front page of the *News Sentinel* and all three local network television stations this morning."

"That means the phone will be ringing in a little while and we'll be covered up by the media. We need to notify the Sheriff," I said.

"That's probably already been done. He was going into his office carrying the paper when I knocked on your door. He didn't look happy."

"Let's go to his office and get this over with," I said.

We paused outside Sam's door and heard him speaking loudly.

"You're *supposed* to be a journalist. If you really were, you wouldn't have posted that video without checking in with us.

"If you had, you could have reported that Larry Wilkin took early retirement yesterday—at my suggestion.

"We didn't approve of what he was doing, and when we found out what he was doing, acted immediately!"

"Don't throw the First Amendment right of freedom of religion at me after what you've done!" We heard Sam slam the receiver down.

I pushed the door open a crack and said, "Is it safe to come in, Boss?"

"Sure, why not? Just give me some good news because it's not eight o'clock yet and I've already had a week's worth of bad news."

"Sam, just let the phone ring. Holly will take messages until Madeline gets here. Then Madeline can handle them. She's an old pro."

"I'm not *that* old!"

"Sorry, Madeline, I didn't see you come in," I said meekly.

"What shall I tell them, Sam?" Madeline is a sturdy woman, pushing sixty and a force to be reckoned with.

"Tell them to call our Public Affairs Office. We still have a Public Affairs officer, don't we?" Sam said.

"Yes we do. I briefed her yesterday on the Wilkin departure and told her to give no comment when news of his death leaks out. You ought to know by now reporters *always* call your main line first before they call Public Affairs. They hope you'll start babbling—and you probably did."

"Sorry, Madeline. I'll be good," Sam replied.

Neither Al nor I were surprised by the deference Sam paid Madeline. Good secretaries, not executives, run the world.

"See that you do, and one of you men make yourself useful by turning on the coffee maker. I set it up before I left yesterday."

Al and I both started across the office to comply with her instructions, but Sam was closer.

"One of these days, she'll get me straightened out," Sam said, "and don't you sneer at me, Holly already has you half-trained. Coffee will be ready in five minutes. One of you, make yourself useful. Get the clean cups and cream and sugar. And get Madeline a cup—light cream, no sugar."

We had moved to the conference room and Sam had calmed down considerably. Just as we were settling in, Holly came in carrying a plate of assorted Danish pastries, and turned on the coffee maker. I waited until she left the room before speaking.

"How do I get a raise for my secretary? She goes beyond and above what I expect of her."

"I don't know," Sam said, "I'm just the sheriff. Do you know, Al?"

"Take your request to Chief Wittaker in Personnel and he'll give it to the Sheriff to approve," Al said.

"*Really?*" Sam said.

"Don't you read what you sign?" I asked.

"I'm not a detail person," Sam said. "Madeline reads it before I sign it."

"Are we going to call Lieutenant Freed in for this meeting?" Al asked. "I think it would be a very good idea."

"I told Madeline to have him come up about ten minutes ago," Sam said.

"I can't believe Chief Hodge got to the media so quickly," Sam said. "I was going to hold a press conference early this morning and get out ahead of it."

"It would probably still be a good idea to have it." I said. "Ethyl Wilkin said she wouldn't talk to the media before telling us, but it's not something that's going to stay secret very long."

"That's why I told Madeline to set it up for eleven o'clock," Sam said. "I'll need you and Al and John to be there, but I'll take the questions so John doesn't have to talk."

Just as Sam stopped speaking there was a knock on the door.

"Come in, Lieutenant," Sam said.

John entered and looked in our direction.

"Madeline said you wanted to see me, Sheriff. Is there a problem?"

"No, John, we're about to have a discussion on the Wilkin case in preparation for a press conference at eleven, and we all need to be there. I know you don't drink coffee but there are soft drinks and milk in the little fridge. Help yourself."

John looked at the pastries on the table, walked to the office refrigerator, got a carton of milk, and sat down.

"John, before we go any further, I know you feel like you've been excluded from your own case, but you haven't.

"You are the *lead* detective, coordinating everything we find out. We all understand the pressure you're under because the Reverend Bart Wilson was not only your pastor but also a close personal friend, so we're doing the heavy lifting for you when we can. Understood?"

"Yes, Sheriff. I understand," John said. "Would you pass the pastries to me? I haven't had breakfast."

Sam picked up the pastry tray and handed it to John. "Let's get our coffee, then catch John up on the details from last night. John, leave some pastries for the rest of us."

The press conference was held in Sam's office. The sheriff, Al, myself, and John were standing against the wall behind a portable podium as the reporters gathered on the other side of the room. When it appeared that everyone expected was there, Sam stepped up to the podium.

"Ladies and gentlemen," Sam said, "I am here to give a statement and to answer questions I know you have. You want to kick it off, *Knoxville News Sentinel* reporter?"

Bill Mosheim, a veteran reporter in a suit and tie, stepped forward.

"Sheriff, is it true that former Sergeant Larry Wilkin took his own life yesterday, and if so, why is it being kept a secret?"

"Nothing is being kept a secret. The medical examiner and ambulance attendants have all filed reports, as have my deputies. It's a common courtesy we extend to all families of a deceased person to hold back details until all family members have been contacted.

"Former Sergeant Larry Wilkin was found deceased yesterday evening," Sam said, "and we will have nothing further to say until all family members have been notified.

"Uh, Sheriff... we contacted the deceased's wife and she said she has nothing to say at present. This is beginning to look like a cover up," Mosheim said.

"You probably have also contacted the funeral home, the morgue, the sheriff's janitorial crew, and everyone else you can think of," I was almost yelling. "And they *all* told you family members had not been notified. Why don't you show a little *common courtesy and human decency, for once?*"

Everyone fell silent and Sam glanced at me from the corner of his eye. I had broken protocol like an amateur at his first press conference, and I had no idea where the rage had come from.

"Chief Tempest has given you the final word on former Sergeant Wilkin's death until all notifications have been made," Sam said. "Channel 10, do you have a question?"

"Yes, I do" An attractive blonde news anchor familiar to most of us stepped forward.

"Is it true that Sergeant Wilkin was the pastor of a church called the Sanctified Gospel Temple and was preaching homophobic sermons and you asked him to resign when you found out?"

"When it came to our attention that *former* Sergeant Wilkin was preaching what we perceived as hate-mongering that might have affected his veracity as a witness in cases he had prosecuted. I *offered* him the opportunity to take early retirement and keep his pension and benefits."

"Paul Johnson Channel Six News, Sheriff. Would it be fair to say he left under pressure?"

"He decided it was in his best interests to take early retirement. He turned in his signed papers and was accompanied to personnel by Chief of Detectives Al Reagan, where his retirement was witnessed and approved by the proper authorities.

"I don't know how I can make this any plainer. Thank you, ladies and gentlemen, for meeting with us. That will be all."

The members of the news media left, unsatisfied as usual, and I took the opportunity to duck out and head to the Chief of Personnel's Office. I found him engrossed in some kind of report in his small office.

"May I interrupt, Chief Wittaker? I have a question."

He looked startled for a second, then answered with a smile. "Of course, sir. Come on in and close the door. Just have the one extra chair in front of my desk, but you're welcome to it."

"I see you're busy, so I won't take up much of your time." I closed the door and sat down.

"How can I help you, Chief?"

"I want to give my secretary, Holly Sowers, a merit raise, and the Sheriff said to see you."

Wittaker turned in his seat and tapped the keys on his computer, then looked closely at the screen.

"Miss Sowers got a small raise at the first of the year..." Wittaker began.

"Everyone got a small raise at the beginning of the year. I want to show her how much I appreciate her efficiency."

"I'll dig you out a pay scale sheet for clerical employees and a wage request form. Of course, the sheriff will make the final decision."

"That sounds good," I replied.

As he searched for the proper forms, I took a look at the photographs on his wall.

"You have a lot of pictures of your military service, Chief Wittaker."

"Most of the Vietnam War photography was done on cheap cameras and couldn't be blown up. Either that or we depended on military photographers who sometimes tossed us a nice shot they had made."

"That's true," Whittaker said, "The Afghanistan and Gulf Wars were well documented."

"You Gulf War Army vets had better hats, too. In my day we were still wearing those cheesy baseball caps for casual wear most of the time. What do you call this hat?" I pointed to a photo of Wittaker sitting at a table with several other soldiers.

"Mostly, we just called them boonie hats. They were comfortable and gave good cover from the sun."

"I only saw them on Special Force units working with units from Australia in 'Nam. I guess they have become pretty standard today."

"They were during my service days," he said. "Here are the forms you need, Chief. After you fill them out, have the Sheriff sign off and he'll pass the finished product to me."

"Thanks, Chief," I said on the way out. He didn't answer, though, but seemed to be absorbed in whatever he was reading before.

EIGHTEEN

"*Holly, will you* come in here, please?" I said into the intercom.

"On my way, Chief Tempest."

A moment later, smile on her face, my young secretary entered my office.

"A couple of things, Holly: I need to reach an Army Major named Vincent Ogden. You don't need a pad; I already have it written down.

"Two years ago, he was in the First Brigade chain of command in Baltimore, and he could have been transferred or even retired, but Baltimore is a place to start."

"All right," she said.

"After you do your check, write down his current location and number and delete all traces of your inquiry," I said and watched the expression change on her face as what I had said sank in.

"Chief..." she began.

"If you can't do it in good conscience, just say so. I know you're not supposed to do it, but I can't have somebody in records notice and ask why I was trying to reach an Army Recruiting officer."

"I understand," she said. "It must be important or you wouldn't ask me to do it."

"The outcome of a case I'm working depends on being able to ask for a discreet inquiry from a man I've personally known for over 25 years."

"Then consider it done," Holly said. "Is there anything else, Chief Tempest?"

"Yes, I just put you in for a merit raise and I wanted to tell you in advance so it would not look like I was trying to influence you. It's a done deal. You'll get the rest of the information from your promotion papers as soon as the Sheriff signs them."

"I wasn't expecting it, Chief Tempest."

"It's a *merit* raise based on superior service. It's been on my mind for a while now and I just got around to it. I don't suppose I need to tell you that for the sake of your relationship with your colleagues, it's better if you keep it to yourself."

"No, we can be real *bitches*," she said. Her face immediately flushed. "I mean..."

"I know what you mean, Holly. Thank you."

"Thank *you*, Chief. I'll get right on this."

I leaned back in my chair and loosened up my back muscles with a shrugging movement.

I was feeling pretty good about myself. I had been able to get a raise for an efficient young woman, just because she deserved it—not always the reason men my age promoted pretty young women, but the reason young women become so distrustful of the system.

My cell phone played the theme song from *The Sting* and I saw it was John Freed on the other end.

"What's up, Lieutenant?"

"Patrol just brought Todd Aiken in. I think he's off his meds. An officer stopped him a few blocks from your house and had to call for backup. He's injured two officers."

"How are the two officers, John?"

"They both walked into the Emergency Room under their own power, but the two that brought him in are pretty banged up, too."

"I'll be right down, John."

I put my pistol in my desk drawer with a sigh. *Maybe Jennifer was right. Some people are too broken to be redeemed.*

I rode the elevator down, assaulted by the smell of urine, flatulence, and disinfectant. You get used to the smell when you're here every day, but I had done my time as a corrections officer long ago.

The elevator door hissed open and I saw John and two patrol officers standing outside the holding cage where Todd Aiken was cuffed and in leg chains. He had a black eye and his shirt was in shreds. The two patrol officers didn't look much better.

"Tell them to open the cage," I said.

"Chief, he's wild," one of the patrol officers said, "even cuffed and manacled."

"Tell them to open the cage." The officer did as he was told and the doors slid open. I stepped in and signaled the corrections officer to close it back.

"Don't get up, Todd."

He looked up at me angrily but remained seated. I walked past him and sat down on the bench.

"You off your meds, Todd?"

"Don't need no fuckin' meds," he told me.

"Yes, you do, just like a diabetic needs insulin. The last time you went off your meds, you decided Freemasons were plotting against you and tried to kill me twice. Do you remember that, Todd?"

"I don't believe that about Freemasons anymore. I was just patrolling your neighborhood when the cop stopped me. I tried to explain I was working for you, but he wouldn't listen."

"Todd, the last thing I told you was to stand down and stay out of the way so we didn't have any more misunderstandings.

"Now you've assaulted and injured police officers trying to do their duty. We have to decide whether to let the VA take another shot at helping you or to charge you with multiple felonies and send you into the prison system. We no longer have hospitals for the criminally insane."

"Prisons *are* the mental hospitals now! If he had just *listened* to me none of this would have happened."

The former Army Ranger gave me a hateful stare and I saw he had a cut over the eye that wasn't bruised. I started to speak again, but instead took a deep breath and signaled for the jailer to open the cage. When I was outside and Todd Aiken was locked down again, he yelled at me once more.

"You're not gonna leave me here, are you, Chief, after everything I've done for you?"

John Freed and two officers stood waiting to see what I would do next.

"Who is the arresting officer?" I asked.

"I am, Chief," a short, stocky officer replied. "I'm willing to work with you if you don't want him put into the system."

"Officer..." I leaned forward and looked at his name tag "...*McCarthy*. Charge him with every applicable violation.

"After he sits in a hospital cell for awhile and he's back on his meds—*if* he takes his meds—maybe he'll come around. But I doubt it and I won't have *anybody* injuring officers of this department."

"Will do, Chief," McCarthy said. "If you change your mind, I'll work with you."

"I appreciate that, Officer. Come on, Lieutenant Freed, let's go get some coffee."

"Are you *really* going to leave me down here?" Todd Aiken yelled as John and I walked to the elevator. "I was working for you, damn it! You said I had *redeemed* myself."

When the elevator door closed, John said, "I know you have a soft spot for veterans, Chief..."

"I do, John, but I can't risk having him hurt our officers."

"Why are you so down, *jefe*? When a New York Steamer from Firehouse Subs with enough corned beef brisket, pastrami, and provolone to slow down the average man's heart while still eating it doesn't make you feel better, it has to be bad."

Magdala came over, laid her head in my lap, looked up with sad eyes, and whimpered.

"Knock it off, Magdala," Jen said. "Shiloh knows the difference between real sympathy and someone who is trying to con him out of part of his sandwich."

My German shepherd gave me one more sad look and whine, cast a glare at Jennifer, then collapsed on the floor beside the kitchen table with a sigh.

"It does smell delicious. Did you get me any extra peppers?"

"Of course I did *mi amor*, and a bag of jalapeño potato chips and a large cookie for dessert. And with my very own hands I brewed us Java Tilu Mountain coffee, which we haven't had before."

"You do spoil me," I said, unwrapping my sandwich, which had been cut in two, then taking a bite, I chewed slowly, savoring the mixture of tastes.

"Delicious, *mi amor*. What are you having?"

"A salad with chicken," she said.

Magdala whimpered to remind us she was not having *anything* delicious, but we ignored her.

"Now, Shiloh, what is troubling you?"

"You remember Todd Aiken?"

"How could I forget him?" Jennifer took a bite of her salad, raising her eyebrows.

"He was patrolling our neighborhood when one of our officers recognized him and pulled him over. He got violent, sent two officers to the hospital with fairly minor injuries, and banged up two others before they got him cuffed and shackled."

"He's a *dangerous* man, Shiloh—and off his meds, I presume?"

"Yes." I took a sip of the Java Mountain coffee and it seemed to have a slight taste of cinnamon. "Good coffee."

"Where is Todd Aiken now?"

"He's in a psychiatric holding cell at the Maloneyville Road facility."

"Waiting to be transported to the VA hospital from which he was just released?" Jennifer asked.

"No. He's waiting for a hearing, charged with several violent felonies."

"No doubt, though, the arresting officer has agreed to cut Aiken a break if you ask him to give the man who tried to kill you another hospital vacation?"

I took another bite of my sandwich, chewed and swallowed, then took another sip of coffee.

"So, judging by your silence, the subject has already come up?" Jen leaned forward with anger in her dark eyes.

"It came up, but I didn't bring it up. I told the officer to charge Aiken with every applicable violation."

"Was that all that was said?"

"Well, John Freed did mention that I had always had a soft spot for veterans after we left the jail…"

"John said that? What in the hell is he thinking?"

"He just saw how upset I was and was more or less making conversation, Jen. He wasn't *suggesting* I do it."

"Listen closely to these names, Shiloh: David Berkowitz, Jeffrey Dahmer, Dean Corll. Do those names ring a bell?"

"Of course they do: Dahmer the Cannibal; Berkowitz, the Son of Sam; Corll, The Candy Man. They were all serial killers."

"They had something else in common, Shy—they were all *honorably discharged* U.S. Army veterans."

"They were *insane*, Jennifer. This is not the same type of situation."

"The difference is that the Army *recognized* that Todd Aiken was broken and let him go, but nobody picked up on the other three until they became monsters. *Some people can't be fixed, Shiloh!*"

"Why do you know so much about serial killers?" I asked.

"I'm a lawyer and the cases came up in my studies. Don't try to change the subject."

"I'm not changing the subject. I just can't see Todd Aiken as *that* kind of monster."

"*Mi amor*, you believe in redemption. And it's a *good* thing, but some people can't be fixed. You can't see Todd Aiken as a monster because in your mind he's a part of the warrior ethic you hold onto so dearly. But this man is now a threat to you, me and all your friends—more dangerous than some serial killers because of his skills.

"Let it go, Shiloh. You have to let it go."

NINETEEN

Holly was waiting in my office when I arrived at work the next morning. She had prepared a cup of coffee and had acquired a cheese Danish somewhere.

"When you are ordering the Danish, be sure and give me receipts so it isn't coming out of your own pocket, Holly. It does look delicious, though."

"Don't worry about it, Chief. Major Vincent Ogden, now Colonel Ogden, called before I left yesterday, but I decided it could wait until this morning. He's now the director of Reserve Officers Training at a small college in Atlanta, but he's at a conference in Pigeon Forge this week. Here's his telephone number at the hotel. He said he'll be waiting for your call."

"Very good, Holly."

"Chief, I got my letter this morning from the Sheriff's secretary."

"That's good, I knew it was on the way, Holly."

"Chief, you promoted me *two* grades. I'm now an *Executive Secretary*!"

"Well, you work for an executive, Holly. I thought it was appropriate that you got paid for it."

"I just wanted to say thanks, Chief."

"Holly, you *earned* your promotion. I didn't do you a favor, I just recognized your talent and dedication. If you're thinking about hugging me, it would be a violation of personnel rules."

"I know, so I'll give you a *virtual hug*." She blushed and left the room.

It occurred to me that I had never had a virtual hug before. I smiled and reached for the paper she had given me with Vince Ogden's number and punched it into my cell phone. He answered on the second ring.

"Vince, good to hear from you."

"You too, Shiloh. You've become a famous writer since the last time we talked. You said you would and you did. And you're also the Chief Deputy for the Knox County Sheriff's Office. Impressive, my friend,"

"Don't blow smoke up my ass, Vince. I'm still who I always was. A lot of my old friends contacted me when I had the first *New York Times* bestseller, but you didn't."

"What, and be accused of sucking up to a celebrity? I've read all your books, though."

"Just kidding, Vince. But as you can see, I'm not too proud to ask for help when I need it."

"Just how may I be of service, old friend?"

"Maybe not at all, Vince, but if not it's good to connect again."

"Spit it out, Shiloh."

"Vince, do you still have connections with your old buddy who was in Criminal Investigations Division when we were at Fort Bragg?"

"Warrant Officer Tony Torralba?"

"Yeah, he's the one."

"We are still in touch. He's retired, but I can probably get almost anything you want through my friends in recruiting."

"This has to be under the table, Vince. The guy I'm investigating is smart and probably has a lot of old military connections, and is in a position to check any official requests I make."

"Well, it sounds like Tony would be the best alternative. Give me the intel on your guy."

"Why don't you send me your cell phone number and I'll text the information to you, Vince."

"You think your target may be *that* good?"

"Probably not. Just being cautious. I know it's going to take a while, but if you're going to be in town a couple of days, maybe I can drive up and buy you lunch."

"Shiloh, this is the age of computers and instant communication. You text the information to my cell phone, and if it's to be had at all, a couple of hours is all I need. How about lunch at the Grand Resort Hotel and Convention Center on the Parkway this afternoon? That way you don't have to pay—I have an expense account."

"I can be there, Vince."

"All right. Are you ready to copy my cell phone number?"

"Go ahead, Vince..."

I got on to I-75 northbound headed for Sevier County, a forty-five-minute drive, where Sevierville, Pigeon Forge, and Gatlinburg are located.

Once Gatlinburg had been the premier destination in Sevier County, billed as "Gateway to the Smoky Mountain National Park," the most visited national park in the United States. However, after a Sevier County native named Dolly Parton opened Dollywood in Pigeon Forge, it caused a major change in local dynamics.

Gatlinburg continued to be a thriving resort town, and the once tiny city of Sevierville had prospered with the growth around it after Dollywood became a major destination for tourists.

After all, who doesn't like Dolly Parton, whose local fans had a statue erected in her honor in Sevierville?

Once all the businesses in the three rural cities had pretty much shut down in the winter, but these days tourists find themselves in heavy traffic the year round, and today was no exception. Traffic was already backed up at the I-75 exit to the three cities when I arrived.

I took a deep breath and told myself to relax and enjoy the drive.

Pigeon Forge is the place where Jennifer and I spend our unofficial anniversary of the day we met, when she was twenty, coming out of a bad marriage and a student at the University of Tennessee, and I was a thirty-eight year old Sergeant with the Knox County Sheriff's Office, working an extra job, directing traffic at a street construction site.

There's nothing inherently exciting in Sevier County except excellent food, dozens of souvenir shops to browse through, and a wonderful bookstore across the street from a small family-owned motel called the Norma Dan, where we stay whenever possible.

There's a joke among locals that when you are in Pigeon Forge or Gatlinburg, you will always see someone you know but haven't seen in decades, even though you have lived in the same city most of your lives. It's a popular place, especially for lovers.

Eventually, as I enjoyed the scenery and memories, the Grand Resort Hotel and Convention Center came into sight. Jen and I had stayed there once when the Norma Dan was filled up, but the place was too busy for us that day with a troop of Girl Scouts in and out all night.

There was plenty of parking, so a few minutes later I entered the spectacular main lobby and was about to ask someone where the dining area was.

"Hey Shiloh. You're holding up well for a short stocky cop. Hair is still dark—or is it natural—and you still look fit."

Truthfully, I would not have recognized Vince Ogden had I not been expecting him. His once muscular build seemed to have settled around his waist and there was little left of what had once been a bushy brush-like blond mat of hair, even when cut in a military style.

"Vince, you old dog, you haven't changed a bit."

"Liar," he said, grabbing me in what passes for a hug among cops and soldiers— shaking my right hand and putting his left around my neck, but patting me hard on the back to show it was comradely affection among tough guys. In our younger days, American cops and soldiers didn't hug at all.

"Come on, I've reserved us a table." He nodded at the doorman, who pointed to an empty table.

"You want a beer or a cocktail, Shiloh? Never mind, you're on duty, so coffee or something soft?"

"Coffee will do nicely," I said. "It really is good to see you."

"Have a seat, Shiloh. I've got all the intel on your guy. And maybe more than you wanted. I caught Tony Torralba when he was bored to death with retirement. It turned out, it wasn't his case but he had been briefed on your guy as a backup witness because it was a high-profile case. Very interesting stuff. But let's order first." I had forgotten about Vince's tendency to skip from one point to another without warning.

"Suits me, Vince."

"I had lobster last night, but the filet mignon is to die for, though you'll need two if you plan on filling up."

"Lobster and filet mignon? Man, you've come a long way since officer candidate school, Vince."

"Well, I did go on to get a master's degree in military science, and I'm spending the college's dime. Did you ever get a college degree after OCS, Shiloh? "

"No, never had the patience. I was busy *doing* things, Vince."

"Yeah, like becoming famous and rich?"

"More of the first and less on the latter. The big money in writing books comes when someone makes a movie or television series from one of your books."

"Really? I thought all bestselling authors were rich. Here's our waiter. Juan, I'll have two filet mignons, rare with mushroom gravy, a baked potato, and macaroni and cheese. And bring me a couple bottles of Heineken Dark to start with."

"Don't overdo it on green vegetables," I said.

"Colonel Ogden is not a big fan of vegetables," the waiter, who appeared to be Latino but with perfect English diction, said, jotting down the order.

"What may I get you, sir?"

"The New Orleans style Cajun pasta looks good," I said, "with a fruit bowl on the side, and coffee to drink."

"That's all you're gonna have?"

"That's it, Vince. How do you think I stay at my fighting weight?"

"Will that be all, sir?" Juan asked.

"Yes, thank you, Juan."

"Shiloh, this subject you needed the intel on," Vince said as the waiter walked away, "was a hell of a soldier. Did you know he has a Purple Heart and a Silver Star?"

"I did not."

"He was also a Ranger and the youngest Master Sergeant in his unit during the Second Gulf War, with an impeccable record."

"Was he also a trained sniper?"

"Yes, familiar with every weapon in the arsenal. Why do you ask, Shiloh?"

"When did things go bad for him, Vince?"

"He had a son, who apparently intended to follow in his footsteps, and enlisted before the Second Gulf War at eighteen. Signed up for advanced infantry training.

"Afterwards, he went to Fort Bragg for airborne training and did well. While he was on a three-day pass, waiting for reassignment, he was picked up in a sting operation by the Charlotte Police for soliciting a prostitute."

"And it wasn't a *female* prostitute he solicited, was it, Vince?"

Vince's eyes narrowed. "No, it was a male prostitute. But you already suspected it didn't you?"

"I did. What happened next?"

"'The kid was released to the Provost Marshal at Fort Bragg and he was restricted to barracks.

"Out of courtesy, his father was notified and he took leave time and headed for Fort Bragg.

"When the young soldier found out his father knew what had happened and was on his way there, he hanged himself off the upstairs back porch of his barracks."

"Damn," I said. "Talk about a moral conflict between a father and son."

"The authorities covered it up for the old man's sake, but professional soldiers, especially high-profile guys, have no real secrets," Vince said. "He had to have been humiliated."

"So he resigned?" I asked.

"No, he went back to work and apparently started a one-man campaign against gay soldiers and the places they frequented off post. Bear in mind, we were still at war in Iraq and Afghanistan and in need of good soldiers—and the prevailing culture was 'don't ask, don't tell.' But this guy was relentless in his crusade against gay soldiers. There were even allegations that he was quietly encouraging violence against gay individuals," Vince said, taking a long swallow from the Heineken Juan had quietly set on the table along with my coffee.

"Eventually he was brought up on a General Court Martial for insubordination."

"*General* Court Martial. That should have come up on his police background check as a felony," I said.

"If they had gone through with it, it would have," Vince said, "but the Army takes care of its own. He was a twenty-year veteran with a Purple Heart and a Silver Star, so they let him take retirement."

"And left the mess for somebody else to clean up. I'm becoming familiar with the pattern," I said.

"It's come up before in your career?"

"It has. By any chance do you know where he was stationed when this near court martial happened?" I asked.

"He was at Fort Gordon, Georgia, awaiting another combat assignment."

"The nearest city to Fort Gordon is Augusta, right?"

"I think so, Shiloh. I saw a light go on when I told you where his last post was. So this intel is useful?"

"I believe it will take me where I need to go, Vince. If it does, I will owe you big time."

"Just out of curiosity, if this guy is so savvy, how did you get on his trail, Shiloh?"

"I saw a picture of him in uniform during the Second Gulf War and he was wearing a 'boonie hat,' which caused me to wonder how he would look in a gray fedora."

"*What?*"

"It's a long story, Vince, and I see our food is coming. Remind me that I have a couple of my first edition books in the trunk of my cruiser for you. Man, that New Orleans style Cajun pasta looks good, especially the shrimp."

TWENTY

It was dusk when I approached the city limits of Knoxville, quitting time for day shift cops who were not on salary. I still had to clean up my desk.

As always, I was a bit startled when my cell phone rang out *The Sting*. I pushed the button on my phone, which is mounted on a holder.

"This is Tempest, go ahead."

"You must be in the car, *mi amor*, where you can't see your cell phone screen."

"Yes, I am, *mi compañera*. How may I be of service?"

"Do you think it would be possible for you to stop at Billy's Burgers on your way home without creating a disturbance? I'm craving one of their mushroom burgers and I want to eat with you tonight when you get home."

"I think I can manage that. Onion rings on the side?"

"Yes, and don't forget to buy Magdala a child's burger."

"Consider it done, Jennifer Mendoza."

"Thanks, Shy. *Te amo*"

The phone went dead before I could reply, and just as I reached the exit for the City-County Building.

Upstairs, the hallways were empty except for Records Division and in my office. When I opened the door, Holly was preparing my coffee machine for the next morning. She appeared startled when I opened the door.

"Chief Tempest, I wasn't expecting you back today."

"I see you're still staying late, Holly."

"How was your trip to Pigeon Forge, Chief?"

"Very productive, Holly. Also caught up on old times with a friend and had a great meal."

"Well, I'll say good night then..." but she paused at the door, looking undecided.

"Is there something else, Holly"

"I just wondered, is there anyway someone could have found out I deleted the call I made to your friend?"

"I don't think so, Holly, but I'll check tomorrow with someone who knows more than I do about computers. Has someone said something to you about it?"

"No, but I had to go to records twice this afternoon and Chief Whittaker came out of his office and *stared* at me both times."

A thrill ran through me, but I didn't let Holly see it had disturbed me. I *would* check with someone tomorrow who knows more about computers than I do.

"You're an attractive young woman, Holly. I'm sure a lot of men stare at you."

"Not *him* and not the way he was looking at me—like I was an insect he wanted to step on."

"Holly, I promise you this, no harm will come to you or your job security, even if someone should find out what happened. I ordered you to do it and *my* boss, who has the last word, won't mind if I have to explain it to him."

"All right, Chief. It may have been my imagination. I'm not much of a rebel. I never once cut a class all through high school and college. Have a good evening."

"You, too, Holly."

I pulled into the lot of Billy's Burgers, making sure to park in a proper space. As I approached the building, I saw the chubby assistant manager with whom I had the altercation standing near the back. I walked over to see what I had done wrong this time.

"Detective Tempest..."

"*Chief* Tempest," I said.

"Chief Tempest, we're being robbed by the guy in the blue hoodie. He's making the clerks go on with taking orders, but he took our cell phones and sent me back to open the safe and I came out the back to see if I could get help."

"Blue hoodie, you say? Did he show a weapon?"

"He let me see it, but he's holding it under his jacket. He's as cool as a cucumber—like he's done it before."

I handed the assistant manager my cell phone. "Call 911 and tell them I need backup. Wait about a minute and come from the back holding a money bag."

"He could shoot me..." the man said.

"I won't let that happen. While he's focused on you, I'll enter and take him down from behind."

"You gonna shoot him?"

"I'm going to take him down. *Move!*" I watched the assistant manager go around the building as he made the call on my cell phone, and slowly made my way towards the door.

I removed my collapsible baton, generally called an *Asp*, from my jacket pocket, shook it out to its sixteen-inch length, and held it to the side of my leg.

I was breathing hard. *Let's do it one more time, Shiloh Tempest—nobody lives forever*, I thought—then pushed the door open as I saw the man in the blue hoodie look to the rear of the store.

I was under an adrenaline rush, but I was certain that nobody looking at me would see anything but an aging man entering to get some take-out food.

When I was eighteen inches from the man in the blue hoodie, I saw that he was around five feet eleven, maybe a hundred and eighty pounds.

As he focused on the approaching assistant manager, I jabbed the tip of metal baton up under his shoulder blade, hard, and leaned into him to speak at the same time.

"I am a police officer and if you move, the next sound you hear will be a bullet taking out your heart. *Stand still.*"

I heard a sharp intake of breath as he tensed up and waited for his next move. He did not move.

"Smart criminal," I said. "You may live through this after all. Now, very slowly take your pistol out with your left thumb and index finger and gently put it on the counter in front of you. If I even *suspect* you're about to try and draw it to use, I will shoot. *Do you understand?*"

"I understand," he croaked out.

"Then do it, slowly."

He raised his left hand and showed me his thumb and index finger in an exaggerated manner and slowly lowered his hand to his waist line.

I thought it was going to end peacefully until I saw his jaw, barely visible from where I stood, clench. He might as well have told me he was going to try and draw his weapon.

I stepped a little to the side and struck him across his left wrist and heard the bone break. At the same moment he screamed in pain and collapsed.

While he was writhing on the floor, I leaned down and took a cheap nine-millimeter pistol from his waist band.

"*Moron*," I said into his ear.

"Man, look at all the cop cars," said a customer sitting at a table eating his food, apparently unaware of what had been happening. There were two Knox County Sheriff's cruisers and one from the Knoxville Police Department.

As the officers exited their cruisers and cautiously approached Billy's Burgers, I showed them my badge though the glass windows. One of the county deputies recognized me and spoke to the other two. They holstered their weapons and entered.

As they came in, the tall blond deputy who had recognized me, said, "Damn, Chief Tempest. Couldn't you have left us something to do?"

"You're welcome to cuff him and transport, but be careful—I broke his wrist with my baton. Also, I need three warrants because I don't have any with me. I'll fill them out while I wait on my food."

The big deputy nodded towards the cruisers, signaling to a smaller deputy who had followed him in, apparently to get warrants, then took out his cuffs.

The Knoxville city officer stepped up and helped him lift the still sobbing armed robber off the floor. I heard the KPD officer mumble under his breath to the big deputy, "Man, your chief is a cool old dude."

"*Owwwwwww*," the man screamed. "My arm's broke. This is *brutality!*"

"I doubt you know what brutality means," the blond deputy said as he lifted the armed robber from the floor. "But the boys at the penitentiary will teach a pretty lad like you *everything* they know about brutality."

The hoodie had fallen away and I saw for the first time that the bandit I had just captured was probably no more than twenty years old, with a complexion as fair as John Freed's and red hair to match.

"Chief, what did you want to take out?"

It was the pretty girl I had talked to on my last trip to Billy's Burgers. She smiled and motioned for me to come to the counter.

I realized she was the clerk being held at gunpoint and secretly admired her composure.

"I need a mushroom burger, a jalapeño burger, and a child's burger, plain. Also, two orders of onion rings. You needn't hurry, I'll be here filling out and signing warrants for a few minutes."

"Don't worry, Chief, we'll keep your food warm." She showed me dimples and wrote down my order.

The assistant manager with whom I had once had problems chimed in, "Chief, I'm Willy Gordon, assistant manager—whatever you want from now on is on the house."

"I appreciate that, Mister Gordon, but I'm not allowed to accept gratuities." He beamed, apparently at being called "Mister."

Damn it feels good to be a knight in shining armor, basking in glory again!

Now all I had to do was explain to Jennifer how it was I stopped for food at Billy's Burgers and interrupted an armed robbery.

Holly came into my office with a cheese Danish as I was finishing my first cup of coffee.

"You're all over the news today, Chief."

"I saw the messages on my desk, Holly, from all the reporters who have called."

"Have you answered any of them?" she asked.

"No and I don't intend to."

"You should. You've made us all look good. Even my father called me this morning with a message for you," she said with a smile.

"What did your father say, Holly?"

"He said, 'Tell your boss I'm glad to see that there's still fire in the furnace, even though there's a little snow on the roof.'"

"Thank your father, Holly. That definitely makes me feel young and vigorous at my age."

"It was a compliment, Chief," she said taking my coffee cup to refill it.

"I know it was, but I just wasn't expecting it."

"Also, the Sheriff is on his way in here." She paused and listened. "He's knocking right now. I'll be leaving."

"Come in," I said,

Sam entered, wearing a charcoal-colored suit, a pale yellow shirt, a black silk tie with blue embroidery, and his two-tone saddle oxford shoes.

"Get your story ready, Shiloh. We'll be having a news conference at ten."

"You don't sound happy, Boss," I said.

"I'm not happy, *Chief Deputy*. Afterward, I'll want you to explain to me why you walked into an armed robbery without backup, apparently armed only with a collapsible baton."

"I *had* my handgun, Sam, but I didn't want to touch off a shooting match in a room full of civilians."

"Maybe I was wrong in not sending you for a psychological exam when your friends and roommate told me your behavior was becoming bizarre, including going into a cage alone with that lunatic Todd Aiken! Last night, *one* misstep on your part could have cost me my chief deputy and Jennifer a roommate."

He slammed the door on his way out, leaving me thinking that it was not the reaction I expected from an old street cop with whom I once worked the streets. He seemed even angrier than Jennifer when I had tried to explain it to her.

The door opened and Holly came in. "Sounds like the Sheriff is upset with you."

"That he is and I don't really know why."

"Madeline gave me a message for you also," Holly said.

"What did Madeline say?"

"It's kind of embarrassing for me. Do you want to know *exactly* what she said?"

"Go ahead."

"Madeline said to ask, 'What the fuck is wrong with you?' and to remind you you're not twenty-five-years old anymore."

"Well, I guess that makes it unanimous," I said. "*Nobody's* in my corner."

"I'm in your corner Chief, and so is my father. We both think what you did was *heroic*."

"Thank you, Holly. I'm going to need a little while to think. Take note on my calls and tell anyone who wants to come in I'm busy—including John Freed and Al Reagan."

"Whatever you say, Chief Tempest."

The scene in Sam's office, with a temporary podium and a department seal on the wall behind it, was set up as usual, with the usual gang of reporters.

Bill Mosheim, the veteran reporter, as always in a suit and tie; Paul Johnson Channel Six News, wearing a small hat and a ratty trench coat he considered journalistic; and the attractive blonde from Channel 10 news whose name I could never remember. The rest could have been interchangeable.

Sam walked to the podium and said, "Ladies and gentlemen of the press, we appreciate your taking the time to see us this morning, regarding an incident last night at a fast food restaurant on Emory Road, just off I-75 North that involved my Chief Deputy, Shiloh Tempest.

"Since I wasn't present, I'll ask Chief Tempest to step up and answer your questions."

Damn, no set up and no pats on the back. He really is angry!

I walked to the podium and attempted a cordial smile, which in my case very often comes off as a grimace.

"I am open for questions. Let's start with veteran reporter Bill Mosheim from the *Knoxville News Sentinel*."

"Chief Tempest, is it in the job description of the Chief Deputy of Knox County to answer armed robbery calls?"

"Bill, while it is unusual for a Chief Deputy to answer *any* call, I stumbled on to this one while stopping for dinner."

There was a murmur of laughter about the first part of my answer so I continued. "The chief deputy takes the same oath as every other deputy sheriff to enforce the law and protect the public, and I've been a cop a long time. I saw a situation and acted."

There was a brief silence, so I called for the next question.

"Channel 10 news, do you have a question?"

"Yes, Chief," said the attractive blonde whose name I could never remember, "what does it feel like to confront a man armed with a pistol?"

"It's terrifying, but I've acted many times in my life when I was terrified. Courage doesn't mean *unafraid;* it means staying in control and overcoming the fear."

"Is that why you were able to face a man armed with a pistol, when witnesses say you had nothing but a metal baton?" the blonde reporter asked. There was a murmuring from those who had not done their homework.

"I was also armed with a handgun, as required by departmental regulations, but I feared that letting the suspect see it would touch off gunfire, endangering civilians."

"Some might say that your actions were reckless and self-serving," said Paul from Channel 6 News, without waiting to be called on. "Have you discussed this with Sheriff Renfro to see how he feels about it?"

"The incident occurred last night and the Sheriff and I have a conference right after the news media is finished here," I answered.

"Chief Tempest, Ronni Patterson from the *Online Daily News*. I have a question."

"Go ahead, Ms Patterson, I don't believe we've met."

"The *Online Daily News* only started up last week, Chief Tempest, but we have proper credentials."

"I wasn't questioning your credentials. Go ahead with your question."

"I interviewed one of the witnesses, shortly after you left the scene last night. She was the young woman being held at gunpoint when you intervened. This is a direct quote: 'Chief Tempest strolled in here like a hero from a Western movie and took down a dangerous guy with a gun—and never drew his own pistol. Chief Tempest is a *mature* man, I'd like to spend some private time with. He's my hero from now on.'

"Would you care to comment on the young woman's statement Chief Tempest?" the reporter asked.

The room erupted in laughter, probably because of the expression on my face.

"Go ahead, Chief," the Channel 6 reporter said, "tell us how it feels to be lusted after by a sweet young thing."

Sam sat at his desk, staring out the window, and I saw no help was coming from him.

"If there are any *serious* questions left, I'll take them now. Otherwise, I thank you on behalf of the Sheriff for your interest."

Then, before anyone else *could* ask a question, I left with egg all over my face. A lot of people would be enjoying my discomfort all day and probably for a month to come.

TWENTY-ONE

I sat at my desk, smoking a cigarette, trying to bring myself under control. I was startled when Sam entered the outer door without a warning from Holly.

"I told Holly *not* to warn you I was coming and I see you started without me today," Sam said, straddling the chair as always.

"Sam, *two things*—I don't appreciate being hung out to dry in front of the news media and *do you want my resignation?*"

"Shiloh, two things—being embarrassed is sometimes the downside of acting under an adrenaline rush as you did, and if I wanted your resignation, I would have asked for it! Well, *three* things. Give me a cigarette."

I slid my cigarettes and lighter across the desk and waited until Sam lit up and slid them back.

"I've seen you take worse risks a dozen times," I said.

"That was *before* you and I became the adults in the room with a whole department watching us. We're not kids any longer. You're the Chief Deputy of the Knox County Sheriff's Office, not a glory-hungry rookie. I imagine that Jennifer also gave you hell last night because she understands *exactly* what happened. Just like I do."

I couldn't argue with what he said. Jennifer had been so angry that Magdala ran to our bedroom without waiting for her sandwich when her mistress got in my face.

"Did you get anything from your source in Pigeon Forge yesterday?"

"How did you know... never mind. I forgot that I have no secrets."

"Nobody told me anything. I listen to radio traffic and I knew you wouldn't leave town for a casual luncheon with the gravity of the case being worked. Let's have it."

"I went to see an old friend named Vincent Ogden, an Army colonel, now running a ROTC unit at a college in Georgia, who used to be in close touch with a Warrant Officer in the Criminal Investigation Division."

"Did you strike pay dirt?" Sam asked.

"I did. It's all theory now, but I'm convinced that our very own Chief Lance Wittaker is the man in the gray fedora and our shooter."

"Damn, Shiloh. Give me the details."

Sam listened intently as I related what Vince Ogden had told me. When I was finished, Sam sat shaking his head for a few seconds.

"This is a two-cigarette crisis," he said.

We both lit up and sat quietly, our anger for the moment overcome by the idea of solving a difficult case on a long shot.

"That was good detective work," Sam said, "The whole slender thread unraveled because of a picture of Lance Whittaker wearing a military hat during the Second Gulf War that resembled a gray fedora."

"The gut feelings should be followed," I said.

"Agreed, but we don't have a shred of evidence to get a search warrant for Whitaker's home and vehicles."

"My guess is that he has a storage unit, anyway. He's a bastard, but a *smart* bastard," I said.

"So, who are we going to let in on this right now?" Sam asked.

"I say we sit on it and gather more intel. Holly thinks Whitaker knows about my trip to Pigeon Forge, even though I had her delete her contact with Vince Ogden.

"It's a long shot, but she's a savvy young woman and Whitaker *is* in control of the computer system."

"I'll have the kid in the gold-rimmed glasses who set up the equipment when we watched the video before in a few minutes. I can trust him."

"What's his name?" I asked.

"I don't remember off hand, but he owes me personally, big time, for keeping him out of jail when he hacked the wrong computer," Sam said.

"You have eyes and ears everywhere, don't you, Sam. So are the two *of us* good?"

"Yes and yes—but if you pull another cowboy stunt, we will revisit our conversation."

"I copy that, Boss."

Twenty minutes later, the kid in the gold-rimmed glasses showed up at my office and Holly let him in.

"Chief, I'm Russell Freeman. The Sheriff told me to put myself at your disposal."

Russell looked to me to be about fifteen, but so do most young people these days.

His hair was brown and curly, but not very long, and he was wearing a tee shirt that said *I'm not crazy—my Mom had me tested.*

"Did he tell you that nobody else is to know what you're doing?"

"Especially Chief Whitaker, right?"

"Right." *Apparently Sam really trusts this kid.*

"Before we start, I have a question."

"At your service, Chief."

"Is it possible that Whitaker was able to read one of Holly's e-mails after it was deleted?"

"Yes and no. Our system is constantly backing itself up. If old Ramrod knew exactly where, or rather *when* to look, he might have been able to see it *before* Holly deleted it. That would have required perfect timing on his part, though, and that's highly unlikely."

"So he probably didn't know about it?"

"I didn't say that, Chief. There's another possibility and I can check for it in about five minutes by looking at your secretary's computer."

"Then by all means, check it now. Is there any way Whitaker can see what you're doing?"

"No, sir, and even if he saw me working on it, I could just tell him I'm doing random checks for quality control, which I do every day."

"Holly," I spoke into the intercom. "Russell Freeman is going to do a random quality control check on your computer. He has my permission."

A few seconds later, Holly opened the door. "Come on and check it, Mr. Freeman."

While the technician was working on Holly's computer, I looked up the Augusta Georgia Police Department and learned it was located in Richmond County.

I checked the Sheriff's Department and saw that *it* appeared to be the major law enforcement agency in the county.

I called and asked for the ranking officer in the Criminal Investigation Division, and to my surprise I was promptly connected without a wait.

"This is Major John Sully, Criminal Investigations."

"Major Sully, this is Chief Deputy Shiloh Tempest with the Knox County, Tennessee Sheriff's Office. Thanks for taking my call."

"Glad to do it. How about them Tennessee Vols, Chief?"

"How about them Georgia Bulldogs, Major?"

I only knew the name of the Georgia football team because I had read an article about a minor scandal involving the team. I know less about the Tennessee Volunteers, but I had grown skilled at covering my ignorance after decades as a cop in a macho football environment.

"How can I help y'all up there in Knoxville, Chief?"

"I was wondering if maybe you had some unsolved shootings, possibly around late 2001, possibly by a sniper."

"I don't even need to look that up, Chief. I was running a beat then and we had three fatal sniper shootings. Two outside gay bars and one a block from another gay bar. You think you might have our shooter? No statute of limitations on murder. But you already know that."

"It's too early to say, Major, but it's a possibility. Can you send me the case files?"

"Sho will, Chief. I'm sure I have a clerk with nothin' to do. I'll have them copied and faxed to you today."

"If you would, just overnight them to me, Major, marked 'Detective division, Chief Tempest, *personal*.'"

"Playin' this one close to the vest, Chief?"

"Sometimes you can't be too careful, Major Sully. On an unrelated matter..."

"You want to know if I'm related to Captain Sully who landed the plane in the Hudson River and saved all his passengers? Sorry, I'd be proud if I was related but his real name was *Sullenberger*. I get asked that a lot, though."

"Actually, I was going to ask you if you're originally from the South Carolina coast."

"I sure as hell am—from Charleston, but why do you ask?"

"I went through basic training at Fort Jackson, South Carolina, towards the end of the Vietnam War and one of my barrack mates was from Charleston. I'm good with accents and you two sound alike."

"I went through basic at Fort Jackson, too. A few years later, of course."

"Of course. I started young but I am an *old* war horse, Major."

"Don't matter, you done your part. I'll get them files on the way, Chief."

"Thanks, Major Sully."

As I finished my phone call, Holly opened the door and Russell came in.

"Did you find what you were looking for, Russell?"

"I did, Chief. Is Holly married or engaged?" he blurted out. He immediately grimaced, realizing he had stepped over a line.

"You will have to ask Holly that question yourself, Russell. Did you find what you were looking for?"

"Sorry, Chief. I did find a keylogger spyware program in Holly's computer. Everything she types comes up on the screen of whoever installed it."

"How did they get to Holly's computer?"

"They sent her an e-mail and the program installed itself."

"That sounds like someone who knows what he's doing."

"Not really. Keyboard spyware can be bought online for fifty bucks or less and all the buyer has to do is follow directions. Probably even you or the Sheriff could do it. Sorry, Chief, no insult intended."

"Did you remove it?" I asked. I didn't take offense, because I had come to understand that computer people live in their own world by their own standards.

"If I do that, whoever installed it will know you're on to him when he doesn't get any more data."

"Did it come from Whitaker's computer?" I asked. "If it did, it gives us probable cause for search warrants."

"Not from his *office* computer. The data is being transmitted to a private computer and I can't backtrack it. We need to let Holly know it's there. That way, we can feed him bad information—assuming it is Chief Ramrod."

"Why do you call him that?"

"We all do. He walks around like he has a stick up his ass."

"Holly, come in here, please," I said into the intercom.

TWENTY-TWO

As soon as I pulled into the driveway, Magdala's head popped up in the kitchen window and I knew she was barking the doggie equivalent of, "Daddy's home."

I had rescued Magdala from a previous owner when I caught him trying to beat her with a baseball bat. As far as breed standards go, she is what you call sable over tan, or mostly black with few distinct color lines as found in show dogs. But she had paid me back for my rescue of her by saving my life. Our bond is unbreakable.

Jennifer also appeared in the window and looked out, alerted by our German shepherd's distinct vocalization. She waved, appearing to be cordial once more after last night's tantrum.

I had sent a text asking Jennifer to prepare a pot of coffee and stopped at one of her favorite restaurants, O'Charley's. It had been a long day and I was hoping for peace tonight.

I could hear Magdala's nose at the bottom of the door sounding like a vacuum cleaner. She began to whine as she got her first whiff of the food I was carrying, then Jennifer opened the door, dressed in a yellow chiffon nightgown. Almost but not quite see through.

"I come bearing food," I said.

"Magdala, back up and let your weary parent come in. Smells good, m*i amor*."

"I brought you a French dip sandwich and a side of artichoke dip. I have fish and chips, and Magdala has a nice ground round steak."

At the sound of her name, Magdala pushed herself between us as Jennifer leaned in to kiss me.

"Go get out of your work clothes, Shy, while I feed Magdala before she has a breakdown. I'll pour coffee and put our food on the table."

Thank God, I thought on my way to our bedroom, *at least she doesn't appear on the verge of mayhem tonight.*

I toyed with the idea of putting on jeans and a tee shirt, but instead put on a silk maroon bathrobe Jen had bought for me. I had seldom worn it, because I'm just not a bathrobe guy, but tonight it seemed like a good idea. I slipped on a pair of house shoes and went back to the kitchen.

"Have a seat, *muchacho*. Magdala has already wolfed down her hamburger steak and our food is on the table."

"Coffee smells good. What blend is it?"

"It's Folgers French Roast. I haven't been to the import store this week."

"That will do." I sat down and took a sip of the hot coffee. Jennifer had added two artificial sweeteners. "Very good."

"How was your day, *Jefe*?"

"Well, first thing, I was humiliated in front of the news media."

"I caught that clip on the six o'clock news. I'll have to go with you the next time and take a look at the sweet *señorita* who is lusting after you. You looked so *guilty* on television."

"Then Sam came into my office and said if I pull another cowboy stunt, he may send me to see the shrink."

"Did you two snort at each other like two *toros*?"

"No we did not. Sam and I have been friends too long and men who go armed for a living learn not to let things escalate to that point."

"That was it?" she sounded almost disappointed.

"Pretty much, I offered my resignation and he turned it down. Also, I had picked up a lead on a suspect in our sniper case and we both got busy on that and forgot about the argument."

"Do you know who it is?"

"Ninety-nine percent, but we can't prove it yet." I took a bite of my flaky fish and it tasted delicious.

"So, who is it?"

"I can't say. We're juggling facts and besides, talking about the details can jinx the case."

"You're punishing me for last night, aren't you? We've talked about your cases plenty of times."

"Not at this delicate stage. Right now, I know every person who has a clue as to what's going on. If we have a leak, it won't be hard to track down."

"Are you saying I'm a blabbermouth woman who can't be trusted?"

"*God, no*! Eat your sandwich. It's standard protocol in situations like this. Nobody can say something *accidentally* that they don't know." I waited but no explosion came.

"Did you check on Todd Aixen today?"

"No."

"That was too quick, *mi amor*. It's not in your nature to let go of *anything* so easily. Let's hear the rest."

"All right, I called a psychotherapist I know who specializes in violent criminals and asked him to do me a favor. He's going to evaluate Todd and if he says there's no hope, we'll proceed with charges and he'll go into the prison system."

"That's it? You'll abide by what your friend says?"

"I will. I can't endanger you and my fellow officers again. Besides, if Todd's *really* that dangerous, he might try to hurt Magdala.

"*Eres un asno,*" she said. Then in English, "Jackass."

I unlocked the outer door to my office and saw a cherry cheese Danish on my desk and a package from the Richmond County Sheriff's Office. Major Sully had wasted no time in mailing my files.

I took off my jacket and poured myself a cup of coffee, reminding myself to tell Holly she was to stop buying pastries for me.

Sitting at my desk, sipping coffee and eating the Danish, I opened the packet and began to go through the three case files. They were thorough and neatly typed. All three cases were almost identical to the murder of John's pastor.

I picked up my cell phone and called Sam's number. He answered quickly. "Sam Renfro, High Sheriff of Knox County. What do you need, Chief Deputy?"

"Will you come by my office when you have time, Sam?"

"Since you aren't coming to my office, which would be protocol for anyone but you, I'll be there shortly."

"I have material that isn't leaving this office and is going in my secret floor safe when I'm not here."

"One excuse for insubordination is as good as another, Shiloh. Fix me a cup of coffee and break out the ashtray."

When Sam came into my office wearing a three-piece pinstriped suit, his coffee was ready and my cigarettes, battered ashtray, and lighter were on the side of the desk where I knew he would move a chair and turn it around backwards.

After lighting a cigarette and taking a sip of coffee, he picked up the three files I had placed on the desk.

"Before I read these, why didn't I get a cheese Danish? I saw Holly bringing one in here earlier."

"What can I say, Sam? Holly spoils me and I can't make her stop."

"That velvet leash she already has around your neck will tighten a little every day, until she bosses you around the way Madeline bosses me."

He opened the first file and began to look through it.

"Richmond County, Georgia—that's Augusta, right?"

"Whitaker was at Fort Gordon, near Augusta, when the Army forced him out. On a hunch, I called the head of the Richmond County Sheriff's criminal investigation division and hit pay dirt."

"So you did. Good hunch and good detective work. Can we connect Whitaker to any of these sniper attacks?"

"Not yet, but we will."

"*We* will? Are you finally going to turn this over to the Lieutenant in charge of the Reverend Bart Wilson's case?"

"Sam, do you think John could hold it together working in the same building with the bastard that killed his friend and pastor until the case is solid?"

"I don't know, Shy, and I would hate to have John confront him, because one of them would die. But you can't work this by yourself."

"I was considering updating Al. He's steady as a rock."

"Why would I *not* want to have my two top chiefs working a case behind the lead detective's back? What did you find out about the possible leak in the computer system?" Sam asked.

"Russell found out that someone, probably Whitaker, installed a program in Holly's computer that records every keystroke she makes on her computer."

"Enough for a search warrant?"

"No, but enough to feed him false information any time we want to."

"Do I see a plot unfolding in your twisted intellect, Shiloh?"

"Maybe the germ of a plan, Boss."

"Do it right, Shiloh. This treacherous bastard is dangerous. What do Holly and Russell know? We don't want to put them in danger."

"Just that he's been spying on Holly's computer. And I *will* do it right, Sam. But I'll also move as *fast* as I can. You, me, John, and CJ may be in sights next."

TWENTY-THREE

Al sat by my desk, looking through the last of the three files sent to me by Major Sully from Augusta, Georgia.

He put the folders on my desk, took out his pack of lens-cleaning papers, and began to clean his glasses.

I waited for him to go through his ritual, knowing that the synapses in his brain were firing as he absorbed what he had just read. When he was ready, he spoke.

"It's him, Shiloh—or one of the world's most extreme coincidences, and we've both been around too long to believe in coincidences. Lance Whitaker is our shooter.

"The question now is whether to bring John in. He's smart and brave, but he's also passionate and feels responsible for his pastor's death. I can see him confronting Whitaker and touching off a shooting."

"Sam and I are in agreement, Al. We're also in agreement that any of us involved with the wedding or one of our family members may be the next target. Speed is of the essence here."

"It's too bad we're not like Whitaker," Al said. "He could just come to a bad end and we'd never find any clues."

Sam looked me directly in the eye and waited for my response.

"Fortunately, we're *not* like Whitaker, Al. But it doesn't mean corners can't be cut while taking him down."

"Sounds like you may have ideas about how that can be done, Shiloh."

"Whitaker installed a program on Holly's computer that records every keystroke, and while he may suspect it, he doesn't know for sure we're on to him. Psychopaths think they're smarter than everyone else.

"When the time is right, we can feed him messages that will go directly to his laptop computer and nowhere else."

"I see the possibilities, Shiloh. What's the plan?"

"We need somebody to put a bug on Whitaker's private vehicle so we can know where he is at any given moment— somebody who can't be connected to us, Al."

"I have an informant, off the books, who did black ops for the National Security Agency," Al said.

"I suspect that Whitaker has a storage locker or maybe even a second private residence. We need to *discreetly* locate it. He's too smart to store anything really incriminating—say, a sniper rifle—at his home."

"The bug on his car may give us that, but if he's avoiding the place, I have a source in the property assessor's office. If he has more property in this county, it can probably be found pretty quickly."

"We need to get the ball rolling. I think we need to check out an unmarked vehicle and do a little recon on the house where he lives."

"I'll put my informant on the clock and get a quiet property check started. Are you busy this afternoon?"

"I can make time."

"Good. I'll alert my guy at fleet to get us something nondescript and unofficial ready, and meet you there about one this afternoon."

"Do it, Al. I'll be there."

Al Reagan was standing by an old, battered Ford pickup truck when I arrived at the fleet lot. The formerly blue paint job was mottled with rust.

"Talk about nondescript, nobody is likely to pay any attention to this truck where we're going today," I said.

"Whitaker is in his office and I have somebody ready to alert us if he leaves," Al said. "I'll feel more comfortable after we get the bug on his car and can keep up with him. Hopefully, that will be done tonight."

Al fired up the old pickup truck and smoke billowed out of the exhaust.

"The fleet manager says it looks worse than it is," Al said. "He assures me it will get us there and back."

"That's all we need," I said, taking off my sports jacket and tie, leaving only my plaid shirt showing. Al was already wearing a tee shirt and baseball cap. Nothing attracts attention like a mismatched driver and vehicle on an undercover run.

"It's been a while since the two of us did any kind of real stakeout," Al said, pulling off the gravel lot.

"Well, this will be a short run, no peeing in a bottle or slouching down for long periods inside a car," I replied.

A few minutes later we were on I-75, northbound, enjoying the scenery with our windows down.

"You had lunch?" Al asked.

"No, I haven't."

"I was thinking about stopping at the Sonic Drive-In on Merchant for a foot-long hot dog and a cherry limeade," Al said.

"That's very specific, Al. Were you around when most drive-ins actually served a variety of drinks like cherry, lime, and vanilla colas?"

"Just the tail-end before family-run drive-in restaurants started being run out of business by the big chains, Shiloh. I've been a fan of Sonic since they first opened here."

"So, retro and not original?"

"You're a bit older than I am, Chief," Al said.

"You are right there, Al. By all means, let's stop at Sonic. Do they have barbecue sandwiches?"

"Not at present, but they have all kinds of burgers and chicken sandwiches and two versions of dogs, chili cheese and one with onions, pickles, and mustard, I think."

"That second dog sounds good, especially if they have onion rings. I think I'll try a cherry limeade myself."

Sam took the Merchant Road exit off I-75 and the Sonic Drive-In was only a couple of blocks away. It was still early for lunch and there were plenty of slots open.

Within ten minutes, Al and I were feasting on what was almost a drive-in meal from the nineteen fifties or sixties.

"Well, Sonic has a better-quality wiener, probably all beef, than we used to get at neighborhood drive-ins, Al," I said, finishing my hot dog, "otherwise it's very authentic."

"You ready to move on, Shiloh?"

"Yeah, but let's take Central Avenue Pike over to Emory, since we're in no hurry," I said.

"The scenic route it is, Boss. You spent part of your childhood around here, didn't you?"

"I did, and I ran ambulance calls out here in the early seventies. That's why I gravitated back to my current neighborhood."

"A lot of nostalgia, I'm guessing?"

"For sure, Al. I've run emergency calls all over North Knox County."

We drove along in silence for a while, two old warriors looking back, until we turned right on Emory Road and then left on Pedigo Road, where Whitaker's home was located.

"Geez," Al said, I had forgotten how twisted this road is."

"Yep, there are a couple of hairpin turns coming up that are unbelievable. Whitaker's place is just beyond the second hairpin. We can see one side on the first hairpin and the other side on the second hairpin."

"That's it," I said, "the house with a red roof and a ten-foot chain link fence all the way around the yard."

"He's cleared away the brush and shrubs all the way up to the fence and it looks like floodlights all over the place."

"You think your boy can cross all that clear land and get to the car in the driveway?" I asked.

"If anyone can he will. He'll disable the light system and drug the dog, if Whitaker has one. This guy used to break into embassy compounds."

"How much is this guy costing us, Al?"

"About three grand, but I have a healthy slush fund right now. No problem."

"I have my fingers in my ears and I didn't hear what you just said, Al."

"Good idea, Shiloh. The property looks the same on both sides. Do you want to turn around and make another pass?"

"No, just keep going and we'll come out on Norris Freeway. I assume your black ops guy is doing his own recon."

"He may bug the car in the parking lot. Whitaker has the only classic Studebaker that ever parks there."

"The 1958 Golden Hawk. That's Whitaker's car? There were only eight hundred and seventy-eight made that year. It had a 275 horsepower, 289 V8 supercharged engine."

"How do you know so much about it?"

"I always wanted one, but they cost a small fortune."

"When Whitaker first came to the department, he belonged to a vintage car club with a bunch of other cops. So he's had it for a long time. He seldom drives it, but I can't see him taking his patrol car to his secret place because he's too paranoid. Probably thinks the cruiser is bugged."

"It is," I said.

"So, like the old saying goes, just because you're paranoid, doesn't mean you aren't really being stalked," Al said with a smile.

"We're definitely stalking him, Al. So, yeah, that old saying's true in this case."

TWENTY-FOUR

My cell phone woke me up at four-thirty and I saw that the caller was Al Reagan.

"Don't you ever sleep, Al?"

"I do, but apparently our newest Lieutenant, John Freed, doesn't. He was listening to his scanner at three this morning, when a sniper fatally shot a patron at a gay bar off North Broadway as he was leaving the Whirly Gig, a fairly new place.

"John called and said he wanted to rendezvous with the Knoxville Police Department Investigators, since it's their jurisdiction. I couldn't think of a valid reason to say no."

"You were right in giving permission, Al. I'll be on my way to the office in a few minutes."

"What's wrong?" Jennifer asked, as I was getting up, "We haven't had one of ours hurt, have we?"

"No, but KPD just answered a fatal sniper call outside a gay bar off North Broadway where all the renovations are going on. Al wants to get a jump on it this morning."

"You get dressed, *Jefe*, and I'll let Magdala out and brew a pot of coffee." Magdala's head popped up at the end of the bed at the mention of her name.

"I appreciate that, *mi amor*."

By the time I had dressed myself in khaki pants, a plaid shirt and solid tie to match, and a pair of Rockport walking shoes, Magdala came dashing back into the bedroom with her ears up and sat down to stare at me with a puzzled expression.

"Sorry, baby girl, but it's not time for breakfast yet." She collapsed with a loud sigh. Magdala hates breaks in her routine.

As I walked back to the kitchen, Jen handed me a plastic mug of coffee with a lid like a kid's sippy cup, perfect for not spilling hot coffee while driving.

"Good hunting, *señor policía*," she said, kissing me on the lips.

My head was filled with a rush of thoughts as I drove downtown. *Did Al's guy get the bug installed last night so we can nail Whitaker's whereabouts this morning? If not, had he left a clue we could use this time? What if we had a copycat sniper?*

Al Reagan and John Freed were both in the hallway outside my office when I arrived. Al was polishing his wire-rimmed glasses and John was excited and disheveled, hair uncombed, and his tie loosened. He was carrying a folder.

"I expected you would be here by the time we arrived," Al said, as I unlocked my office.

"Pull up chairs while I turn on the coffee. Holly always has it set up."

"Well, John, this is your first break in a case you've spent many hours on." I sat down at my desk, facing the two of them.

"We can look at the paperwork later. Just tell us what you have."

"First of all, you need to thank Tom Abernathy. He showed up at the scene and made sure I got cooperation.

"I have no doubt this was the same shooter who killed Bart. This time he apparently was shooting from the top of a building and the KPD crime techs are looking for his nest.

"It was the same large caliber. This time the round hit a brick wall behind the victim and the round ricocheted across the street. The investigators recovered it, but it's probably too mangled to match." John stopped to catch his breath.

"Now we can be pretty sure this *is* a hate crime."

"Who was the victim?" Al asked.

"Sad case," John said. "He was twenty-six and a teacher at a Baptist private school. When the KPD investigator called his wife, she thought he was out of town and apparently had no idea he had another life she didn't know about.

"The bartender said he was a regular there, but usually only for short visits. Last night he met up with someone who left right before he did, maybe to meet somewhere else. The KPD investigators are trying to locate him."

"Good work, Lieutenant," I said. "Go to your office and make us copies of your file and start a board on this murder, even though it's KPD's case.

"When did you last sleep through the night, John?" I asked.

"It's been a while, Chief."

"As soon as you get organized this morning, go home, have a drink, and go to bed. I can make that an order if I need to."

"Not necessary, Chief. I'm really tired, and now that we have a fresh lead, I may be able to sleep."

When John was gone, I turned to Al.

"Did your boy complete his task last night?"

"He did, Shiloh, but he hasn't activated it yet."

"So we don't know where Whitaker was last night?"

"At ten-thirty, when the bug was attached, both his Studebaker and cruiser were in his driveway."

"That left him plenty of time," I said, "to get where he was going this morning."

"Assuming he was there. We know his cars were both there at ten-thirty, but what if he has another vehicle somewhere and is using a commercial car service like Uber or Lyft when he doesn't want to be tracked?"

"Where would he be keeping another car that would be convenient from headquarters, Al?"

"There are two commercial garages within walking distance of the City-County Building, but the most likely scenario is that he left *after* my man visited him."

"*Occam's razor* states that *of any given set of explanations for an event occurring, the simplest one is most likely the correct one.* You're right, Al."

"After noon today, when I see my guy to complete our financial transaction and pick up his frequency tuner, we'll be able to track both his cars."

"Obviously, he's deliberately rubbing our faces in this, and I suggest we make our move as soon as possible, before he decides to strike again and his next victim is one of us or a family member," Al said.

"I agree. We need to be ready to move when the opportunity presents itself," I said.

It had been a long day. Keeping the operation that Al and I were working behind John Freed's back was a growing strain.

Still, it would just be too dangerous for our new lieutenant to know he was in the building with the man who had killed his friend and pastor and tried to ruin his wedding. Passion and rage can make people forget the consequences of a very bad decision.

No doubt, watching Whitaker walk around the hallways was grating on Al's and Sam's nerves as much as it was annoying me. John Freed just might break under the strain if he knew Whitaker was the shooter.

I pulled into my driveway and movement caught my eye as my headlights lit up the yard. Getting out of my old maroon cruiser, I walked over to see what it was, and froze with anger flowing through me like bile.

It was a piece of stiff wire with a yellow ribbon attached—the kind used by snipers to read the windage when they are setting up for a kill

The bastard had been here in my own yard, a few feet from Jennifer and Magdala. He was *mocking* me, showing he could get to me and my loved ones anytime he felt like it

It's time to end Lance Whitaker, I thought, *before he hurts anyone else.*

Looking up, I saw that Jennifer and Magdala were at the window. Composing myself, I casually pulled up the wire with ribbon on it and carried it to the garage where I tossed it on the floor.

Magdala was dancing around the kitchen when Jen opened the door to the kitchen, trying to vocalize in human words what she was feeling.

"What was that you just pulled out of the ground, Shiloh?" Jennifer asked.

"It's a marker from the utility company. Somebody's probably getting ready to run a new gas line."

"Funny," Jennifer said, "I didn't hear anyone out here. It must have been there when I got home and I just overlooked it. Don't you need to leave it there?"

"No, they will have recorded it electronically by now. The flag was just the preliminary marker."

"If you say so, *señor policía*. Are you hungry? I stopped and got you an order of fried green tomatoes and grits at Puléo's. Magdala and I have already dined."

"You do spoil me, Jennifer." *I really hate to lie to you, but I'm becoming so good at it. Maybe tomorrow, I'll bring this to an end and I won't have to lie to you or John again.*

TWENTY-FIVE

I took a seat at my desk and prepared to eat the cheese Danish Holly had once again brought in, along with the coffee she had poured as soon as I arrived.

Then I called Al on my cell phone and he answered on the first ring. "What do you need, Chief?"

"Can you come to my office?"

"On my way, Shiloh."

I buzzed for Holly and she appeared at the door. "How may I be of service, Chief Tempest?"

"I have something for you." I picked up the envelope I had prepared earlier and held it towards her.

"What is it, Chief?" She took it from my hand.

"It's Danish money. When it's gone let me know, because I've grown fond of my morning treat."

"I can't take it, Chief. After everything you've done for me, a Danish in the morning is not unreasonable."

"The only thing I did for you was see that you got a raise you deserved. You don't say *no* to the Chief Deputy, Holly."

She looked as if she was about to burst into tears.

"Holly, don't start crying, I can't handle it. All you owe me is the superb job you've been doing already."

"All right, you're the boss." Her face brightened up, and at the same moment Al knocked on the door.

"Come in, Al," I said.

He opened the door and came face to face with Holly.

"Good morning, Holly," he said.

"Good morning, Chief Reagan. I was just on my way out."

"Pull up a chair, Chief," I said. "Question—do you know where Whitaker was after work yesterday?"

"Funny you should ask. I was monitoring him, making sure our device was working, and he dropped his cruiser at the service center for an oil lube at five-thirty, and told the mechanic he was going to walk over to Central Avenue and get something to eat.

"He came back an hour later and picked his cruiser up. Why do you ask?"

"Because he has apparently figured out how to be in two places at once. I went home at six thirty last night and there was a ribbon mounted on a wire in my front yard—the kind that snipers use to calculate windage."

"The bastard is taunting me, Al, and I'm going to end it today, if possible."

"He definitely didn't have time to go eat and then get to your house before you got home. Either he had somebody else plant the ribbon in your yard—or he walked around to the fleet lot and got a car there."

"Damn, Al, you're right, and the sonofabitch has succeeded in getting me into a state of mind in which I'm not thinking clearly. That's unusual for me."

"Let's face it, Shiloh. He let you know he could get close to your family without impunity. It would rattle anyone."

"We'll move this evening, but we need to be sure we're following *our* plan and not his," Al said, taking out his little pack of papers to clean his lenses.

"Well, I need to get back downstairs and see what Lieutenant Freed has uncovered. KPD may have turned up something we can use."

As Al opened the door, Sam was about to knock. He said, "Don't run off on my account, Chief Reagan."

"I was on my way down to check on the kids who work for me, Sheriff."

"They do get younger every year," Sam said.

Sam dragged his regular chair in front of my desk and took his cowboy seat. "Do we need a crisis cigarette, Shiloh?"

"Not unless you ask me a question I can't gracefully evade, but you're welcome to a smoke." I pushed my cigarettes and lighter across the desk.

"Whitaker planted a sniper's windage ribbon in my front yard yesterday evening. If possible, we intend to close the case today."

Sam lit a cigarette and said, "He's gone too far."

"He has," I said.

"Do I want to know what's in the works?" Sam asked.

"Not if you want plausible deniability."

"Be careful, Shiloh. It has to *look* right."

"The pieces will fall into place, Sam. We're not going to take him out the way he takes out his enemies. We're cops, not assassins."

"I know you are, or I would have intervened already. I can't have another innocent person killed—especially a friend and colleague.

"How's John doing with his first big lead?"

"He's like a cat playing in catnip. It would be nice if the KPD investigators found a direct connection to Whitaker, but I don't expect it."

"When are you and Al putting your plan that I have no knowledge of in action?"

"Maybe tonight, if the cards fall right, Sam. As you said, he has gone too far."

"Be careful, Hoss. I'm playing golf in a charity tournament today, but you two will be on my mind."

Sam left and I leaned back in my chair, looking out over the Tennessee River and Calhoun's Restaurant.

I lit a cigarette and tried to get the kinks out of my back. I felt like a young paratrooper going out on a recon mission in Vietnam. The possibility of dying never gets any easier, no matter how long you live.

The Sting let me know I had a call. I saw that it was Al on the other end.

"Go ahead, Al."

"How about we walk over to Pete's Restaurant to get a sandwich?" he said.

"A walk would do us both good."

"Sounds good to me. I'll meet you on the main floor and we won't have to walk up the hill to Main Street."

"Be there shortly."

I put on my jacket and went out by Holly's desk. She seemed to be focused on something on her computer screen.

"Holly, I'm going to Pete's. Would you like me to bring you something?"

"I'm tempted, Chief, but I have to watch my girlish figure. Will you be out of the office long?"

"Just a few minutes," I said.

The lobby outside the Sheriff's Office was empty except for two deputies working security. Before smoking was banned, the lobby would have been full of people smoking on breaks, but no longer. One of the deputies turned and saw me.

"Going out, Chief Tempest?" he asked.

"For a little while. Hold down the fort while I'm gone."

I walked across the lobby to the central elevators and punched "M" which actually means *Mezzanine* but had always been called Main. I stepped off the elevator and Al was waiting, polishing his glasses.

We walked in silence across the enclosed bridge to Main Street, but as soon as we were outside, Al said, "Whitaker drove his Studebaker to work today and stopped off at his secret place, and we now have a location about fifteen miles from his house—and I'm familiar with it."

"This is probably the first time since he killed the kid off Broadway that he's felt secure enough to stash his M-14," I said.

"It won't be hard for us to find. The property has an old barn or some other kind of shed. Not much space to hide anything from a skilled searcher," Al said.

"I'd feel better if we had probable cause for a search warrant, but I'm afraid to wait any longer.

"So we'll be doing surveillance because we just found out where his hidden property was, and we'll see him carry the M-14 in, which will give us probable cause since we've been looking for just such a weapon."

"Sounds like a plan to me," Sam said. "The only thing it will take to make it perfect would be if my source in the property assessor's office were to locate it and call me. And since I already know where the property is..."

"It all comes together. We're here at Pete's. Did you really want something to eat or just privacy to talk?" I said.

"I just wanted to talk, but since we're here they have a great Reuben sandwich, among many other fine dishes."

"All right, I'm buying."

TWENTY-SIX

"Holly, will you come in my office, please?" It was *precisely* one hour, as I knew it would be, after she left for lunch when I heard my secretary return and take her seat.

"Yes, Chief Tempest," she said, closing the door behind her "How may I help?"

"Al Reagan and I are going out to do surveillance this afternoon. At some point before you leave today, I will send a text to your phone that says *Now*.

"When you get the text, immediately delete it, then sit down at your computer and type in this message to my e-mail account." I handed her a slip of paper.

She read it carefully, her eyes widening slightly. "You are setting a trap for *him*, because when I type this in he will see it."

"As soon as you have sent the message to my e-mail account, go in and delete it."

"Is this going to be dangerous what you two are doing?" Holly asked.

"Holly, all police work can be dangerous, but Al Reagan and I have about fifty years of experience between us. We plan to send him to the penitentiary for several murders with evidence we will seize today. Timing and secrecy are absolutely critical today if we are to pull it off. We're using a weapon he tried to use against us. Are you up to it? If not we'll call it off because I'm not going to pressure you to do anything you can't do in good conscience."

"If the two of you are willing to go face to face with a monster today, I can at least do my part," Holly said.

"What we are about to do will appear absolutely kosher, Holly, but sometimes we have to bend the rules a little to catch the really sly criminals. The only thing you will know *officially* is that Al and I told you we were going on a stakeout. That's what you will say if anyone asks. We won't let anything touch you."

"So, truthfully, *he* is doing this to himself to cover what he has done to innocent people. I can live with that, Boss. But please *promise* not to let anything happen to you or Chief Reagan." Suddenly, there were tears standing in her blue eyes.

I didn't answer, because nobody knows what will happen on any operation and I wasn't going to lie to her. I just smiled and nodded and she went back to her office.

Al and I had changed into casual clothes, leaving our jackets, dress slacks, and ties in my office.

Al was also wearing a fanny pack, pulled around to the front. I started to make a comment about being over-prepared, but I did not.

Al, however, saw me looking at it and said. "You can put a lot of good stuff in a fanny pack without wearing out your pants pockets."

As we left by way of Holly's office, the Sheriff's secretary, Madeline, was in front of her desk.

"Holly, Al, and I will be out of the office for the rest of the day, doing surveillance on a lead we just got. Just take messages and I'll get to them tomorrow."

"You two worn-out war horses are going to do *surveillance?*" Madeline said. "This won't involve fishing rods will it?"

"No, it's legit. We got a tip that needs to be checked today, and we are available with our fifty years combined experience," I said.

"Does the Sheriff know his two top ranking supervisors are doing grunt work?" Madeline asked.

"I'm sure he will now," I answered. "But the answer is, Sam knows we're working an unusually difficult case that will require everyone getting involved," I said as we left.

We took the back hallway to the parking lot for the Sheriff and his chiefs so as not to raise questions among the staff.

"My car or yours?" Al asked.

"Let's take mine," I said. "Whitaker won't see a vehicle anyway. We'll pull off the road beyond his place and walk in."

"Madeline's presence when we left just added a little more authenticity to our operation," Al said. "I'm beginning to feel lucky."

"Don't jinx us Al. Murphy's law is always in effect. 'Anything that can go wrong, will go wrong.'"

"I know and some people believe Murphy was an optimist," Al said, "but there are sometimes a series of events that make me feel lucky, anyway."

We rode quietly for the thirty-minute trip, two men who had worked together so long that sometimes words aren't needed.

I knew he was experiencing anxiety about what we were going to do, and he knew I was experiencing the same stress. And we were both glad, because a man who is not afraid when he should be will get you killed.

The time passed quickly.

"There's the driveway to his barn or cabin on the left," Al said, looking at the map he had pulled up on his cellphone. "There should be a trail off the highway just ahead, a logging road."

"Sure enough," I said, slowing down. I looked and saw that I would be able to pull my cruiser into the woods without hitting a stump or fallen tree, then eased in about thirty feet off the pavement.

"That went smoothly," Al said. "Let's take a walk."

"Grab my shotgun out of the trunk." I handed Al my keys. "There are five rounds of double-aught buckshot in the cylinder and five more in the sleeve around the stock. If we need more than that, we're in trouble."

It was a twenty-minute walk up the gravel driveway to the clearing where we saw what looked like a small wooden barn or large shed.

It looked shabby but as we got closer, it was obvious that the windows were tightly fitted and that the door was new, with what appeared to be a new lock.

"He has put some money into this place. And he has electricity, Al. Do you want to show off by picking that lock or just break out a window?"

"I can handle the lock," Al said. He took a small leather kit of lock picks from his fanny pack and had the door open in thirty seconds.

"You still got it, Al. I didn't know anybody still carried that kind of tools."

Al stepped back and pushed the door open with his foot, just in case there was a booby trap. When nothing happened, he looked inside the door, reached in, and found the light switch.

"Whitaker has certainly made it convenient for skilled burglars," Al said.

Inside, we found things laid out neatly, as you would expect from an ex-military man. There was a small bed, neatly made, a desk, and a chest of drawers, even a full-length mirror mounted on the back wall, but no plumbing in sight.

"He doesn't spend much time here," I said, "or he'd have indoor plumbing. It's a neat place to go to ground in an emergency, though."

"Where would I be hiding if I were an M-14 sniper rifle?" Al said.

"Behind that mirror, Al. It doesn't belong here—it's out of character with the rest of the room."

Al walked over and peered closely, then ran his fingers around the mirror's wooden frame. He smiled and said, "Bingo!"

He put his right index finger into the slot he had found and the mirror swung out from the wall. Behind it, in a slot just wide enough to hold a rifle, was the M-14 we had been looking for.

"Don't touch it without gloves, Al!"

"I wasn't going to, Boss." Al took a pair of rubber gloves from his pocket, "You keep forgetting I'm the man you made Chief of Detectives."

"Sorry, Al. Smart-asses never get over thinking they're the only people who can do things right."

"John Freed says the same thing about me, Chief." He lifted the M-14 from behind the mirror and examined it.

"Fresh magazine, Shiloh. Shall I unload it?"

"No, just leave it the way it is and hide it under the bed, where our backup will find it in the legal search pursuant to an arrest that will follow after we see Whitaker carry it in and call for help."

"Maybe we can stash it in his car *after* we arrest him, Boss. The idea of leaving this kind of firepower where he might find it, makes me nervous."

"He won't be looking for it, Al. We're going to leave the mirror opened and he'll assume we took it. And we'll interrupt him as soon as he finds the rifle gone."

"You're the boss," Al said, leaning down to push the rifle under the bed. "Guess it's best if only his prints are found on it. We had better take up positions before we put this plan into action."

TWENTY-SEVEN

"You comfy, Shiloh?"

"As comfy as possible sitting in a nest of trampled weeds, Al."

"You ready to send the text?"

"I am." I took out my cell phone, pulled up Holly's number, and entered *Now.*

"The die is cast. In a moment, Holly will send me an e-mail. Which Whitaker will hopefully read."

"He'll read it," Al said." If there ever was an obsessive and compulsive monster, it's him. What exactly will he be reading, anyway?"

"The e-mail Holly is sending to my account says: '*Chief Tempest, meet Chief Reagan at the location of the second property owned by your suspect in one hour and fifteen minutes.*'"

"That ought to do it," Al said. "How about a snack while we wait?"

"Sure," I said, expecting a joke.

Reagan removed two cans of Vienna sausages, a pack of crackers, and two small cans of apple juice from his fanny pack.

"You came prepared, Al."

"If you don't like Vienna sausages, I have a tin of sardines. Juice isn't cold, but it will do."

We opened our Vienna sausages and crackers and began to eat. It's best if you don't think about the ingredients of Vienna sausages while you eat them.

As I was popping open my apple juice, Al's phone rang and he answered it.

"Go ahead, Bro." He listened and then smiled. "Thanks."

"Who was that, Al?"

"It was the parking lot attendant from the City-County Building. Whitaker just tore out of the lot in his Studebaker. Probably thinks he can get here before we do since he doesn't expect us to be here for an hour and fifteen minutes."

"You're probably right, Al."

We finished our impromptu lunch and tried to relax, but Al wasn't any better at it then I was.

After a few minutes, we both took out our Glock pistols and checked to see if the action on them was working properly, as if we hadn't both done it before holstering up that morning.

Al worked the action on my shotgun, cycling a couple of rounds out, then reloading them.

"How long do you think it will take him to get here, Al."

"Thirty minutes tops, which leaves us about fifteen minutes."

Waiting is the hard part when getting ready to go into action. But eventually, it always ends. We heard the powerful V-8 engine while it was probably still a mile away.

"You will take up a position behind *that* tree as soon as he enters the building and I'll move into position to the left of the door."

"We ain't changed nothin' since we made the plan, Shiloh."

"I know, Al, but I'm operating on adrenaline and so are you."

Whitaker's classic Studebaker roared into sight, throwing gravel in all directions and slid to a stop fifty feet from the building.

He jumped from the car, still in uniform, and ran to the door, which we had re-locked. He dug out his keys, threw the door open, and went in, closing it behind him.

Al and I were already in motion as the door closed. Whitaker had stopped his car where I had intended to take up my position so I improvised by taking cover behind the driver's-side fender.

We were prepared for him to run back out when he saw the M-14 was not in his hiding place, but he did not. I saw a curtain move as he peeked out and improvised again.

"Whitaker, come out! You have nowhere to go and we have your M-14. You're outgunned! Surrender!"

The door opened a couple of inches, but he didn't show himself. Instead he yelled back at me.

"You're willing to die, Tempest, protecting the cocksuckers you and Renfro have elevated to places of honor in our department? Is that Chief Reagan behind the tree. I know you both took part in that disgusting abomination you called a wedding, Reagan. You two are no better than the cocksuckers you've allowed to disgrace real men."

"You're a sick man, Whitaker," I yelled. "I know what happened to your son—he preferred death to facing your scorn."

Things went quiet for a moment. My words had not goaded him into charging out.

"So, you've done your homework, Tempest. My son was perfectly straight until some queer turned him into an abomination. They can't reproduce, so they have to seduce. They *all* deserve to die."

"I heard Larry Wilkin use those same words, but you didn't kill him because he was gay. Larry's dead because you were afraid he was going to expose you, so you *murdered* him."

"Larry was weak and was about to put our sacred mission against sodomites in jeopardy."

"Well, your mission ends here, Whitaker. Surrender and live. You'll be a hero in the pen. A mass murderer, a white supremacist, and a homophobic monster all wrapped up in one package!"

"Hey, Tempest, I see you found my warning in your front yard. I shoulda killed that Spanish whore you live with and poisoned that mutt of yours while I was there."

Without warning, the blood was pounding in my head and the rage almost had a taste. The picture Whitaker had just painted consumed all logic and morality from my mind and I began walking towards the door, pistol raised.

"Chief, you're in my line of fire!"

I heard Al yelling at me, but I was beyond reason, consumed with rage. I kept walking.

"Step out here and face me like a man, Wittaker, or I will drag you out of there and rip your throat out!"

"Shiloh, *stop*. You're in my line of fire!"

When I was twenty feet from the door, I saw Whitaker put his arm outside, while peering around the door. He began firing and so did I.

I felt a round hit my right leg, but kept moving. Then, pain seared the left side of my skull and I remembered nothing else that day.

TWENTY-EIGHT

The mechanical sound of machines beeping and hissing and the smell of disinfectant filled my world. Then as I tried to move my arms, I knew I was in a hospital.

I opened my eyes slightly and for a moment was blinded. As my pupils adjusted to light, I saw Sam Renfro sitting in a chair against the wall, reading a magazine.

"Why are my hands tied down?" I asked. "It *pisses* me off to be restrained."

"That would be to keep you from digging at the hole in your skull and ripping out your catheter again, Bubba, when they thought you were too far under to resist. Then you turned your bed over and tried to crawl away You're a lousy patient."

"How long have I been out? Is Al all right? Is Whitaker dead?" My last conscious memories were coming back in a rush.

"Technically, you were out a fairly short time," Sam said, "but the doctors have had you sedated for three days to keep you from hurting yourself.

"Al Reagan is fine. Whitaker is recovering from the ass-whipping Al gave him. One of your rounds hit Whitaker in his left shoulder during your exchange at the door. Whitaker emptied his magazine and Al got to him while he was trying to reload and finish you off.

"Unfortunately, Whitaker's arm was broken and he suffered various bruises and abrasions during the struggle."

"Did Whitaker shoot me in the head? I know I took a round in my right leg."

"No, that thick skull of yours deflected the round that turned what would have been a serious wound in anyone else into what the television writers call a *graze*."

"You said something about a hole in my head, I think, but I'm not really alert."

"I'm going to let your doctor explain that to you. He's here and Jennifer just stepped out to get a report from him. He backed off the sedatives last night and they were expecting you to wake up.

"I'm going to get Jen and the doctor. I'm glad you came through another close call, Hoss. I would have missed our crisis cigarettes." He turned to leave, but I had one more question.

"Sam, have you read Al's report?"

"Oh yeah. Al's source in the assessor's office located a piece of property Whitaker owned. Then the two of you set up surveillance and saw him carry in an M-14 rifle–which was located under his bed—and you had probable cause to believe was the murder weapon. During the course of a legal arrest, there was a shootout, and you know the rest."

"Sam, was there anything else?"

"Not on paper, Shiloh. The reported facts were checked through interviews and everyone from the clerk in the assessor's office to your secretary and mine confirmed the narrative. Of course, Whitaker said he was set up, but who believes a serial killer? It's all copacetic, Shiloh. A righteous bust and shooting."

After Sam left my room, I breathed a sigh of relief. I had never fabricated evidence against an innocent person, but at times events do get out of sequence, say, during an investigation involving a vicious killer.

"Shiloh, my little fighting rooster, it's so good to see you awake." She put her arm around me, firmly but gently, then stood up.

"Shiloh, this is Doctor Hector Sanchez," she said. "He's the one who did your surgery."

"Sam mentioned that I had a hole in my head, then said the round was deflected by my skull. Which is it?" I asked.

"Both," Doctor Sanchez, who turned out to be a tall muscular man with blond hair and blue eyes, despite his Latino name, stepped around so I could see his face. "Your skull *did* deflect the bullet. The hole, as your friend described it, is a very small one I drilled to get a biopsy from your brain."

"This sounds worse all the time," I said.

"No, no" the doctor said. "We did a routine X-ray because, even though the bullet was deflected, it was still high impact.

"The X-ray showed an anomaly, so we did an MRI and found a rather large mass pressing into your frontal lobe on the left side. Your wife gave us permission to do further tests."

"It's good that my *wife* did that." I glanced at Jennifer and she was staring at the wall.

"Yes, it is, there are all kinds of legal hoops to jump through when there's no family. Since the Sheriff of Knox County vouched for Jennifer as your wife, I needed no further proof.

"I could give you all kinds of medical jargon about the mass that only a doctor would understand, but make a long story short, the mass was a cyst, not a tumor.

"When I inserted the needle through the small opening I had drilled for a biopsy, the cyst started draining. I removed all of what was mostly spinal fluid I could with the needle and the next day it didn't even show on our imaging.

"We live in a miraculous time of micro-surgery, Mister Tempest. I was able to make numerous openings in the outside of the fluid sac cyst through the original opening in your skull to make sure it doesn't ever fill up again."

"Is it possible I've been having symptoms and didn't know it?"

"Actually, most cysts of the variety you had never cause any problems. Yours may have been there since infancy until something—we don't know what—caused it to enlarge.

"There are numerous possible symptoms, from headaches, to depression, to having trouble walking. In the most extreme cases, it can cause uncontrollable psychotic-like rage and loss of control over it. Of course those kinds of symptoms would have been noticed by your friends and family."

"So, Doctor, what's the prognosis?" I saw that Jennifer was listening intently.

"We'll keep a watch on you with periodic scans, but I don't expect any further problems. Any symptoms you had should be gone for good."

"We don't know how we'll ever be able to express our gratitude, Doctor Sanchez," Jennifer said.

"Maybe someday I'll need a ticket fixed. Just kidding, I know a man of integrity does not bend rules," Doctor Sanchez said with a smile.

Sam had left and Jennifer was having a cup of coffee. I had been waiting for the expected lecture, so I decided to get it over with.

"Are you going to say *I told you so?*"

"You mean how you sloughed off what all your friends and your loving *compañera* tried to tell you about your recent behavior? No, I hadn't planned on doing that at all. I'm just glad the nightmare is over."

"Excuse me," a nurse stood at the door, "there are two people, a Holly Sowers and a Doctor Craig Schultz out here. Normally only family is allowed in critical care, but Doctor Sanchez told us to make exceptions in your case, Chief Tempest."

"Nurse Gregory, that's very kind. Would you bring in Holly first and tell her she only has five minutes, and tell Doctor Schultz he can come in shortly?"

"I can do that," she said. "I didn't know you had even learned my name, Mister Tempest."

"Shiloh is very good when it comes to noticing pretty young women," Jennifer said.

A minute later, Holly came through the door, ran directly to my bedside, put her head on my chest, and began to weep.

"Chief, I've been *so* worried," she sobbed, "since I heard the shooting go down on the scanner."

"I'm all right, Holly. Just one more scar on an old dog with many scars."

Holly stood, her face streaked with tears, and spoke to Jennifer. "I didn't mean to create a scene... Miss... Jennifer."

"I understand, Holly. Shiloh speaks very highly of you."

"Well, let me wipe the tears away," Holly said, taking out a tissue and patting her face. "The nurse only gave me five minutes and I know there's a doctor waiting to see you. I just had to see for myself that Chief Tempest was all right. I'll be on my way."

"I'm sure Shiloh would appreciate a kiss, Holly, and I don't mind," Jennifer told her.

Holly gave me a quick kiss on the cheek and left the room. We heard her start sobbing again when she was in the hallway.

"That was kind of you, *mi amor*," I said.

"She's very fond of you, in a daughterly sense I'm sure. Besides she looks nothing like Madeline Stowe. By the way, who is Doctor Schultz? And what kind of report does he have?"

"He's the psychotherapist I asked to examine Todd Aiken. Apparently he has a report for me."

"Do you need some privacy, Shiloh?"

"No, please stay."

"May I come in?" Craig Schultz stood in the doorway, dressed like his idea of a shrink, in a tweed jacket with ancient leather patches on the sleeves and a turtleneck shirt.

"Come in, Craig and grab a seat," I said.

"Thank you." He almost bowed in a European manner to Jennifer. "And this must be the lovely Jennifer Mendoza. She really does resemble Madeline Stowe. Sorry, Jennifer..."

"I'm used to the comparison, Craig. Please sit down. Would you like a coffee? It's swill but has caffeine."

"No thanks, I'm on a short break, but I knew Shiloh wanted this report."

Craig took a seat by Jennifer and as soon as I saw his expression, I knew it wasn't going to be an uplifting report.

"Go ahead, Craig. I know you're a busy man and I don't want to take up any more of your time than necessary," I said.

"I didn't need any notes or charts for this one, Shiloh. Todd Aiken has refused his medication at the jail, and has lapsed into his fantasy that he's being persecuted by a worldwide secret organization.

"The delusion, as he has demonstrated, will go away if he takes his medication. But there's no way to guarantee he won't just stop taking it, even if he is stabilized again. In fact, it's almost inevitable he will continue to stop taking his meds in the free world.

"Todd Aiken, in my opinion, is too dangerous to be allowed back in society. I could not in good conscience recommend that the Veterans Administration hospital be given another shot at treating him. He needs to be locked up, sad though it is, where he can't hurt anyone else."

"Would you testify to *that*, Craig?"

"Yes, I would. I'm sorry it wasn't what you wanted to hear, but at the current state of psychiatry, there are still people who can't be fixed."

"Thank you, Craig, for taking the time to give a veteran one final look. If there's any way to repay you, let me know."

"We're pretty even on favors, Shiloh. Jennifer, it was nice to finally meet you. I will be on my way."

When he was gone, Jennifer and I sat in silence for a while.

"I'm sorry," she said. "I know you had grown fond of the young man."

"You have nothing to be sorry for, Jen. You were right all along—not everyone can be redeemed. I'll notify the arresting officer to proceed with prosecution. Valuable lesson learned. And once again, I didn't go out in a blaze of glory," I said, immediately not believing I had just said it.

"What?"

"Just a line from a song Kenny Rogers used to sing back in my younger days."

EPILOGUE

The Reverend Ella Fritz, wearing a blue clerical shirt and collar, in the company of a petite brunette of perhaps thirty, came into our recreation room that we added a while back.

I was sitting in my lounge chair, wearing a blue knit cap to cover the bandage from my recent surgical adventure.

"Shiloh," she said, "this is my wife, Darlene Cumming Fritz. Don't get up."

"Very nice to meet you, Darlene," I said.

"And I'm glad to finally meet you," she replied. "John, CJ, and Ella think very highly of you. Also, I've read your books, all of which seem to feature redemption as a theme."

"Well, I hope you're not disappointed after you get to know me. I'm more intelligent in my books than in real life."

"I doubt that. By the way, I've volunteered as an assistant cook. Who do I see?"

"Ella can take you down and introduce you to Jennifer and the rest of our guests."

"Never mind. I can find my own way down. If you don't feel like coming out, one of us will bring your food up, Shiloh."

She went out through the sliding glass doors and disappeared down the steps from the deck.

"Subtlety is not one of Darlene's strong suits. One of the things I love about her is her childlike approach to life and almost total inability to be deceitful, even in a good cause."

"She's also very attractive," I said.

"Yeah, that too. So what's bothering you, Shiloh?"

"What do you mean?"

"Come on, big guy. John knows something is bothering you and thinks I can help. I'm sure that's why he invited me."

"John is always more perceptive than I give him credit for," I said. "There are a couple of things in your field of expertise that I've had on my mind."

"While we talk, would you mind if we have a Heineken Dark?" Ella said.

"I don't think we have any Heineken Dark..."

"John brought two cold six packs. He knows I like it and he says it's one of your favorites."

"Then by all means, let's do that, Ella. John doesn't drink and I have no idea how he knew about my taste for Heineken Dark."

"I'll get us one," she said. "You don't need a sissy glass, do you?"

Without waiting for an answer, she left the room and returned in just a minute or so with two bottles of the dark Dutch brew.

She put one bottle on the table by my chair and took a seat on the couch across from me behind the coffee table.

"Drink up, soldier, and let's get to talking." She took a long swig, as did I, and carefully put her bottle on a coaster that was on the coffee table.

"Since you're not Catholic or Episcopalian, we can do this like we're old friends having a drink and not as a formal confession."

"Do you believe in free will?" I asked,

"Whoa, bring out the big guns first! Since I'm not a Calvinist, my theological answer is yes. But I have the feeling you're coming from somewhere else."

"I'm not a regular church-goer, Ella, but I've always been geared towards the idea of redemption, and I just had two events in my life that have shaken me to the core."

"Go on," she said.

"I just had a cyst removed from my head that was apparently causing me to behave totally irrationally at times. Was I acting of my own free will when my brain was betraying me?"

"I don't know. What was the other incident Shiloh?"

"I had been working with a Gulf War veteran who was screwed up with what I thought was post-traumatic stress disorder. He tried to kill me twice not very long ago, while under a paranoid delusion, but after being medicated, he came out of the VA hospital, apologized to me, and asked for forgiveness—which I granted when I was convinced that he was sincere."

"Then he went off his meds and reverted. Am I right?" Ella asked.

"Yes. It was like demon possession, if you believe in that sort of thing."

"I'm still up in the sir on that one, Shiloh," Ella said.

"So I got a psychotherapist I trust to examine him, and the therapist informed me that my young friend needs to be locked up for the safety of my officers, friends, and family because he can't be fixed at the current state of psychiatry."

"That's the one that's really bugging you, isn't it, Shiloh? Someone who can't be fixed."

"Yes. How can he have free will when he has no control over himself? Is redemption even possible without free will?"

"I wish I knew the answer to that, Shiloh, but I'm only human and so are you. The protection of society, including your friends and family, from this young man is your responsibility. He exercised free will when he stopped taking his medication. That's all I've got—and it's all you've got."

Strangely, or perhaps not strangely, I felt a burden lift from my shoulders as I listened to Ella's words. She had definitely gotten into the right business for her.

I heard someone coming up the steps and saw Sam Renfro opening the sliding doors. He was wearing a flowery shirt and casual slacks. He nodded at Ella.

"Hoss, are you coming down or do you want your food served up here? We have chicken breast, burgers, hotdogs, plus Bratwurst and Navy beans. And your dog, Magdala, is trying to come up and get you."

"I'm coming down, who all's here, Sam?"

"CJ and John, of course, Al Reagan and his wife, Madeline and her husband, Tom Abernathy and his date, and that gorgeous secretary of yours. Would I be out of line asking Holly out, Shiloh?"

"Not only would it be unethical because you're her boss, but it would also brand you as a dirty old man. Not to mention I think of her almost as a daughter and would feel compelled to defend her honor from an old roué."

"You don't have to beat around the bush, Shiloh. I get the message, and I was kidding anyway. Do you need me to help you down the stairs?"

"No, I'm not ready for the stairs yet. Ella and I will come around from the front. It's a fairly easy walk."

"All right, Shiloh, be advised that the beautiful Latina woman who lives with you just waved for us to hurry."

"We'll be on our way, Sam."

"Meet you out back," Sam said, taking two steps at a time on his way down.

"Are you ready, Ella?"

"Let's go," she said. "It's going to be a good day for you, surrounded by the people who love you most."

"You're right," I said. "Let's get down there before Sam eats all the Bratwurst and beans."

"Should I get us another cold Heineken Dark?"

"Of course," I said, laughing for no obvious reason at all, except things seemed right for the first time in a long time.

ABOUT THE AUTHOR

David Hunter is a retired police detective, a former op-ed columnist for the *Knoxville News Sentinel* for 27 years, the author of 19 books, and of numerous magazine articles from *Jack and Jill* and *Mad Magazine* to *Readers Digest*. He lives in Powell, Tennessee, a suburb of Knoxville, Tennessee, with his wife, Cheryl. He is an inductee into the East Tennessee Friends of the Library Hall of Fame and holds a lifetime achievement award from the Knoxville Writers' Guild. His books have been nominated for the Edgar and Best Appalachian Book Award.

CPSIA information can be obtained
at www.ICGtesting.com
Printed in the USA
BVHW070715120121
597521BV00001B/68